I0535234

The Short Stories Of Rabindranath Tagore, Volume 1

The short story is often viewed as an inferior relation to the Novel. But it is an art in itself. To take a story and distil its essence into fewer pages while keeping character and plot rounded and driven is not an easy task. Many try and many fail.

In this series we look at short stories from many of our most accomplished writers. Miniature masterpieces with a lot to say. In this volume we examine some of the short stories of Rabindranath Tagore.

And with him we venture to the East. To meet the poet and story teller who speaks a common language of love and mysticism which continues to convey valuable insights into universal themes in contemporary society.

Rabindranath Tagore (1861-1941) who was a gifted Bengali Renaissance man, distinguishing himself as a philosopher, social and political reformer and a popular author in all literary genres. He was instrumental in an increased freedom for the press and influenced Gandhi and the founders of modern India.

He composed hundreds of songs which are still sung today as they include the Indian and Bangladesh's national anthems.

His prolific literary life has left a legacy of quality novels, essays and in this volume his shorter works.

Gitanjali, one of his most famous works, earned him the distinction of being the first Asian writer to receive the Nobel Prize in Literature in 1913.

At the end of the poems you will find a longer biography of Tagore, specially written for this volume.

Many of the poems are also available as an audiobook from our sister company Portable Poetry. Many samples are at our youtube channel http://www.youtube.com/user/PortablePoetry?feature=mhee   The full volume can be purchased from iTunes, Amazon and other digital stores. Among our readers are Shyama Perera and Ghizela Rowe

Index Of Stories

The Home Coming

Phatik Chakravorti was ringleader among the boys of the village. A new mischief got into his head. There was a heavy log lying on the mud-flat of the river waiting to be shaped into a mast for a boat. He decided that they should all work together to shift the log by main force from its place and roll it away. The owner of the log would be angry and surprised, and they would all enjoy the fun. Every one seconded the proposal, and it was carried unanimously.

But just as the fun was about to begin, Makhan, Phatik's younger brother, sauntered up, and sat down on the log in front of them all without a word. The boys were puzzled for a moment. He was pushed, rather timidly, by one of the boys and told to get up but he remained quite unconcerned. He appeared like a young philosopher meditating on the futility of games. Phatik was furious. "Makhan," he cried, "if you don't get down this minute I'll thrash you!"

Makhan only moved to a more comfortable position.

Now, if Phatik was to keep his regal dignity before the public, it was clear he ought to carry out his threat. But his courage failed him at the crisis. His fertile brain, however, rapidly seized upon a new manoeuvre which would discomfit his brother and afford his followers an added amusement. He gave the word of command to roll the log and Makhan over together. Makhan heard the order, and made it a point of honour to stick on. But he overlooked the fact, like those who attempt earthly fame in other matters, that there was peril in it.

The boys began to heave at the log with all their might, calling out, "One, two, three, go," At the word "go" the log went; and with it went Makhan's philosophy, glory and all.

All the other boys shouted themselves hoarse with delight. But Phatik was a little frightened. He knew what was coming. And, sure enough, Makhan rose from Mother Earth blind as Fate and screaming like the Furies. He rushed at Phatik and scratched his face and beat him and kicked him, and then went crying home. The first act of the drama was over.

Phatik wiped his face, and sat down on the edge of a sunken barge on the river bank, and began to chew a piece of grass. A boat came up to the landing, and a middle-aged man, with grey hair and dark moustache, stepped on shore. He saw the boy sitting there doing nothing, and asked him where the Chakravortis lived. Phatik went on chewing the grass, and said: "Over there," but it was quite impossible to tell where he pointed. The stranger asked him again. He swung his legs to and fro on the side of the barge, and said; "Go and find out," and continued to chew the grass as before.

But now a servant came down from the house, and told Phatik his mother wanted him. Phatik refused to move. But the servant was the master on this occasion. He took Phatik up roughly, and carried him, kicking and struggling in impotent rage.

When Phatik came into the house, his mother saw him. She called out angrily: "So you have been hitting Makhan again?"

Phatik answered indignantly: "No, I haven't; who told you that? "

His mother shouted: "Don't tell lies! You have."

Phatik said suddenly: "I tell you, I haven't. You ask Makhan!" But Makhan thought it best to stick to his previous statement. He said: "Yes, mother. Phatik did hit me."

Phatik's patience was already exhausted. He could not hear this injustice. He rushed at Makban, and hammered him with blows: "Take that" he cried, "and that, and that, for telling lies."

His mother took Makhan's side in a moment, and pulled Phatik away, beating him with her hands. When Phatik pushed her aside, she shouted out: "What I you little villain! would you hit your own mother?"

It was just at this critical juncture that the grey-haired stranger arrived. He asked what was the matter. Phatik looked sheepish and ashamed.

But when his mother stepped back and looked at the stranger, her anger was changed to surprise. For she recognised her brother, and cried: "Why, Dada! Where have you come from? "As she said these words, she bowed to the ground and touched his feet. Her brother had gone away soon after she had married, and he had started business in Bombay. His sister had lost her husband while he was In Bombay. Bishamber had now come back to Calcutta, and had at once made enquiries about his sister. He had then hastened to see her as soon as he found out where she was.

The next few days were full of rejoicing. The brother asked after the education of the two boys. He was told by his sister that Phatik was a perpetual nuisance. He was lazy, disobedient, and wild. But Makhan was as good as gold, as quiet as a lamb, and very fond of reading, Bishamber kindly offered to take Phatik off his sister's hands, and educate him with his own children in Calcutta. The widowed mother readily agreed. When his uncle asked Phatik If he would like to go to Calcutta with him, his joy knew no bounds, and he said; "Oh, yes, uncle! " In a way that made it quite clear that he meant it.

It was an immense relief to the mother to get rid of Phatik. She had a prejudice against the boy, and no love was lost between the two brothers. She was in daily fear that he would either drown Makhan some day in the river, or break his head in a fight, or run him into some danger or other. At the same time she was somewhat distressed to see Phatik's extreme eagerness to get away.

Phatik, as soon as all was settled, kept asking his uncle every minute when they were to start. He was on pins and needles all day long with excitement, and lay awake most of the night. He bequeathed to Makhan, in perpetuity, his fishing-rod, his big kite and his marbles. Indeed, at this time of departure his generosity towards Makhan was unbounded.

When they reached Calcutta, Phatik made the acquaintance of his aunt for the first time. She was by no means pleased with this unnecessary addition to her family. She found her own three boys quite enough to manage without taking any one else. And to bring a village lad of fourteen into their midst was terribly upsetting. Bishamber should really have thought twice before committing such an indiscretion.

In this world of human affairs there is no worse nuisance than a boy at the age of fourteen. He is neither ornamental, nor useful. It is impossible to shower affection on him as on a little boy; and he is always getting in the way. If he talks with a childish lisp he is called a baby, and if he answers in a grown-up way he is called impertinent. In fact any talk at all from him is resented. Then he is at the unattractive, growing age. He grows out of his clothes with indecent haste; his voice grows hoarse and breaks and quavers; his face grows suddenly angular and unsightly. It is easy to excuse the shortcomings of early childhood, but it is hard to tolerate even unavoidable lapses in a boy of fourteen. The lad himself becomes painfully self-conscious. When he talks with elderly people he is either unduly forward, or else so unduly shy that he appears ashamed of his very existence.

Yet it is at this very age when in his heart of hearts a young lad most craves for recognition and love; and he becomes the devoted slave of any one who shows him consideration. But none dare openly love him, for that would be regarded as undue indulgence, and therefore bad for the boy. So, what with scolding and chiding, he becomes very much like a stray dog that has lost his master.

For a boy of fourteen his own home is the only Paradise. To live in a strange house with strange people is little short of torture, while the height of bliss is to receive the kind looks of women, and never to be slighted by them.

It was anguish to Phatik to be the unwelcome guest in his aunt's house, despised by this elderly woman, and slighted, on every occasion. If she ever asked him to do anything for her, he would be so overjoyed that he would overdo it; and then she would tell him not to be so stupid, but to get on with his lessons.

The cramped atmosphere of neglect in his aunt's house oppressed Phatik so much that he felt that he could hardly breathe. He wanted to go out into the open country and fill his lungs and breathe freely. But there was no open country to go to. Surrounded on all sides by Calcutta houses and walls, he would dream night after night of his village home, and long to be back there. He remembered the glorious meadow where he used to By his kite all day long; the broad river-banks where he would wander about the livelong day singing and shouting for joy; the narrow brook where he could go and dive and swim at any time he liked. He thought of his band of boy companions over whom he was despot; and, above all, the memory of that tyrant mother of his, who had such a prejudice against him, occupied him day and night. A kind of physical love like that of animals; a longing to be in the presence of the one who is loved; an inexpressible wistfulness during absence; a silent cry of the inmost heart for the mother, like the lowing of a calf in the twilight;-this love, which was almost an animal instinct, agitated the shy, nervous, lean, uncouth and ugly boy. No one could understand it, but it preyed upon his mind continually.

There was no more backward boy in the whole school than Phatik. He gaped and remained silent when the teacher asked him a question, and like an overladen ass patiently suffered all the blows that came down on his back. When other boys were out at play, he stood wistfully by the window and gazed at the roofs of the distant houses. And if by chance he espied children playing on the open terrace of any roof, his heart would ache with longing.

One day he summoned up all his courage, and asked his uncle: "Uncle, when can I go home?"

His uncle answered; "Wait till the holidays come."But the holidays would not come till November, and there was a long time still to wait.

One day Phatik lost his lesson-book. Even with the help of books he had found it very difficult indeed to prepare his lesson. Now it was impossible. Day after day the teacher would cane him unmercifully. His condition became so abjectly miserable that even his cousins were ashamed to own him. They began to jeer and insult him more than the other boys. He went to his aunt at last, and told her that he had lost his book.

His aunt pursed her lips in contempt, and said: "You great clumsy, country lout. How can I afford, with all my family, to buy you new books five times a month?"

That night, on his way back from school, Phatik had a bad headache with a fit of shivering. He felt he was going to have an attack of malarial fever. His one great fear was that he would be a nuisance to his aunt.

The next morning Phatik was nowhere to be seen. All searches in the neighbourhood proved futile. The rain had been pouring in torrents all night, and those who went out in search of the boy got drenched through to the skin. At last Bisbamber asked help from the police.

At the end of the day a police van stopped at the door before the house. It was still raining and the streets were all flooded. Two constables brought out Phatik in their arms and placed him before Bishamber. He was wet through from head to foot, muddy all over, his face and eyes flushed red with fever, and his limbs all trembling. Bishamber carried him in his arms, and took him into the inner apartments. When his wife saw him, she exclaimed; "What a heap of trouble this boy has given us. Hadn't you better send him home?"

Phatik heard her words, and sobbed out loud: "Uncle, I was just going home; but they dragged me back again,"

The fever rose very high, and all that night the boy was delirious. Bishamber brought in a doctor. Phatik opened his eyes flushed with fever, and looked up to the ceiling, and said vacantly: "Uncle, have the holidays come yet? May I go home?"

Bishamber wiped the tears from his own eyes, and took Phatik's lean and burning hands in his own, and sat by him through the night. The boy began again to mutter. At last his voice became excited: "Mother," he cried, "don't beat me like that! Mother! I am telling the truth!"

The next day Phatik became conscious for a short time. He turned his eyes about the room, as if expecting someone to come. At last, with an air of disappointment, his head sank back on the pillow. He turned his face to the wall with a deep sigh.

Bishamber knew his thoughts, and, bending down his head, whispered: "Phatik, I have sent for your mother." The day went by. The doctor said in a troubled voice that the boy's condition was very critical.

Phatik began to cry out; "By the mark! three fathoms. By the mark, four fathoms. By the mark." He had heard the sailor on the river- steamer calling out the mark on the plumb-line. Now he was himself plumbing an unfathomable sea.

Later in the day Phatik's mother burst into the room like a whirlwind, and began to toss from side to side and moan and cry in a loud voice.

Bishamber tried to calm her agitation, but she flung herself on the bed, and cried: "Phatik, my darling, my darling."

Phatik stopped his restless movements for a moment. His hands ceased beating up and down. He said: "Eh?"

The mother cried again: "Phatik, my darling, my darling."

Phatik very slowly turned his head and, without seeing anybody, said: "Mother, the holidays have come."

The Kingdom Of Cards
I

Once upon a time there was a lonely island in a distant sea where lived the Kings and Queens, the Aces and the Knaves, in the Kingdom of Cards. The Tens and Nines, with the Twos and Threes, and all the other members, had long ago settled there also. But these were not twice-born people, like the famous Court Cards.

The Ace, the King, and the Knave were the three highest castes. The fourth Caste was made up of a mixture of the lower Cards. The Twos and Threes were lowest of all. These inferior Cards were never allowed to sit in the same row with the great Court Cards.

Wonderful indeed were the regulations and rules of that island kingdom. The particular rank of each individual had been settled from time immemorial. Every one had his own appointed work, and never did anything else. An unseen hand appeared to be directing them wherever they went, according to the Rules.

No one in the Kingdom of Cards had any occasion to think: no one had any need to come to any decision: no one was ever required to debate any new subject. The citizens all moved along in a listless groove without speech. When they fell, they made no noise. They lay down on their backs, and gazed upward at the sky with each prim feature firmly fixed for ever.

There was a remarkable stillness in the Kingdom of Cards. Satisfaction and contentment were complete in all their rounded wholeness. There was never any uproar or violence. There was never any excitement or enthusiasm.

The great ocean, crooning its lullaby with one unceasing melody, lapped the island to sleep with a thousand soft touches of its wave's white hands. The vast sky, like the outspread azure wings of the brooding mother-bird, nestled the island round with its downy plume. For on the distant horizon a deep blue line betokened another shore. But no sound of quarrel or strife could reach the Island of Cards, to break its calm repose.

II

In that far-off foreign land. across the sea, there lived a young Prince whose mother was a sorrowing queen. This queen had fallen from favour, and was living with her only son on the seashore. The Prince passed his childhood alone and forlorn, sitting by his forlorn mother, weaving the net of his big desires. He longed to go in search of the Flying Horse, the Jewel in the Cobra's hood, the Rose of Heaven, the Magic Roads, or to find where the Princess Beauty was sleeping in the Ogre's castle over the thirteen rivers and across the seven seas.

From the Son of the Merchant at school the young Prince learnt the stories of foreign kingdoms. From the Son of the Kotwal he learnt the adventures of the Two Genii of the Lamp. And when the rain came beating down, and the clouds covered the sky, he would sit on the threshold facing the sea, and say to his sorrowing mother: "Tell me, mother, a story of some very far-off land."

And his mother would tell him an endless tale she had heard in her childhood of a wonderful country beyond the sea where dwelt the Princess Beauty. And the heart of the young Prince would become sick with longing, as he sat on the threshold, looking out on the ocean, listening to his mother's wonderful story, while the rain outside came beating down and the grey clouds covered the sky.

One day the Son of the Merchant came to the Prince, and said boldly: "Comrade, my studies are over. I am now setting out on my travels to seek my fortunes on the sea. I have come to bid you good-bye."

The Prince said; "I will go with you."

And the Son of Kotwal said also: "Comrades, trusty and true, you will not leave me behind. I also will be your companion."

Then the young Prince said to his sorrowing mother; "Mother, I am now setting out on my travels to seek my fortune. When I come back once more, I shall surely have found some way to remove all your sorrow."

So the Three Companions set out on their travels together. In the harbour were anchored the twelve ships of the merchant, and the Three Companions got on board. The south wind was blowing, and the twelve ships sailed away, as fast as the desires which rose in the Prince's breast.

At the Conch Shell Island they filled one ship with conchs. At the Sandal Wood Island they filled a second ship with sandal-wood, and at the Coral Island they filled a third ship with coral.

Four years passed away, and they filled four more ships, one with ivory, one with musk, one with cloves, and one with nutmegs.

But when these ships were all loaded a terrible tempest arose. The ships were all of them sunk, with their cloves and nutmeg, and musk and ivory, and coral and sandal-wood and conchs. But the ship with the Three Companions struck on an island reef, buried them safe ashore, and itself broke in pieces.

This was the famous Island of Cards, where lived the Ace and King and Queen and Knave, with the Nines and Tens and all the other Members, according to the Rules.

III

Up till now there had been nothing to disturb that island stillness. No new thing had ever happened. No discussion had ever been held.

And then, of a sudden, the Three Companions appeared, thrown up by the sea, and the Great Debate began. There were three main points of dispute.

First, to what caste should these unclassed strangers belong? Should they rank with the Court Cards? Or were they merely lower-caste people, to be ranked with the Nines and Tens ? No precedent could be quoted to decide this weighty question.

Secondly, what was their clan? Had they the fairer hue and bright complexion of the Hearts, or was theirs the darker complexion of the Clubs? Over this question there were interminable disputes. The whole marriage system of the island, with its intricate regulations, would depend on its nice adjustment.

Thirdly, what food should they take? With whom should they live and sleep ? And should their heads be placed south-west, north-west, or only north-east? In all the Kingdom of Cards a series of problems so vital and critical had never been debated before.

But the Three Companions grew desperately hungry. They had to get food in some way or other. So while this debate went on, with its interminable silence and pauses, and while the Aces called their own meeting, and formed themselves into a Committee, to find some obsolete dealing with the question, the Three Companions themselves were eating all they could find, and drinking out of every vessel, and breaking all regulations.

Even the Twos and Threes were shocked at this outrageous behaviour. The Threes said; "Brother Twos, these people are openly shameless!" And the Twos said: "Brother Threes, they are evidently of lower caste than ourselves! "After their meal was over, the Three Companions went for a stroll in the city.

When they saw the ponderous people moving in their dismal processions with prim and solemn faces, then the Prince turned to the Son of the Merchant and the Son of the Kotwal, and threw back his head, and gave one stupendous laugh.

Down Royal Street and across Ace Square and along the Knave Embankment ran the quiver of this strange, unheard-of laughter, the laughter that, amazed at itself, expired in the vast vacuum of silence.

The Son of the Kotwal and the Son of the Merchant were chilled through to the bone by the ghost-like stillness around them. They turned to the Prince, and said: "Comrade, let us away. Let us not stop for a moment in this awful land of ghosts."

But the Prince said: "Comrades, these people resemble men, so I am going to find out, by shaking them upside down and outside in, whether they have a single drop of warm living blood left in their veins.

IV

The days passed one by one, and the placid existence of the Island went on almost without a ripple. The Three Companions obeyed no rules nor regulations. They never did anything correctly either in sitting or standing or turning themselves round or lying on their back. On the contrary, wherever they saw these things going on precisely and exactly according to the Rules, they gave way to inordinate laughter. They remained unimpressed altogether by the eternal gravity of those eternal regulations.

One day the great Court Cards came to the Son of the Kotwal and the Son of the Merchant and the Prince.

"Why," they asked slowly, "are you not moving according to the Rules?"

The Three Companions answered: "Because that is our Ichcha (wish)."

The great Court Cards with hollow, cavernous voices, as if slowly awakening from an age-long dream, said together: "Ich-cha! And pray who is Ich-cha?"

They could not understand who Ichcha was then, but the whole island was to understand it by-and-by. The first glimmer of light passed the threshold of their minds when they found out, through watching the actions of the Prince, that they might move in a straight line in an opposite direction from the one in which they had always gone before. Then they made another startling discovery, that there was another side to the Cards which they had never yet noticed with attention. This was the beginning of the change.

Now that the change had begun, the Three Companions were able to initiate them more and more deeply into the mysteries of Ichcha. The Cards gradually became aware that life was not bound by regulations. They began to feel a secret satisfaction in the kingly power of choosing for themselves.

But with this first impact of Ichcha the whole pack of cards began to totter slowly, and then tumble down to the ground. The scene was like that of some huge python awaking from a long sleep, as it slowly unfolds its numberless coils with a quiver that runs through its whole frame.

V

Hitherto the Queens of Spades and Clubs and Diamonds and Hearts had remained behind curtains with eyes that gazed vacantly into space, or else remained fixed upon the ground.

And now, all of a sudden, on an afternoon in spring the Queen of Hearts from the balcony raised her dark eyebrows for a moment, and cast a single glance upon the Prince from the corner of her eye.

"Great God," cried the Prince, "I thought they were all painted images. But I am wrong. They are women after all."

Then the young Prince called to his side his two Companions, and said in a meditative voice; "My comrades ! There is a charm about these ladies that I never noticed before. When I saw that glance of the Queen's dark, luminous eyes, brightening with new emotion, it seemed to me like the first faint streak of dawn in a newly created world."

The two Companions smiled a knowing smile, and said: "Is that really so, Prince?"

And the poor Queen of Hearts from that day went from bad to worse. She began to forget all rules in a truly scandalous manner. If, for instance, her place in the row was beside the Knave, she suddenly found herself quite accidentally standing beside the Prince instead. At this, the Knave, with motionless face and solemn voice, would say: "Queen, you have made a mistake."

And the poor Queen of Hearts' red cheeks would get redder than ever. But the Prince would come gallantly to her rescue and say: "No! There is no mistake. From to-day I am going to be Knave!"

Now it came to pass that, while everyone was trying to correct the improprieties of the guilty Queen of Hearts, they began to make mistakes themselves. The Aces found themselves elbowed out by the Kings. The Kings got muddled up with the Knaves. The Nines and Tens assumed airs as though they belonged to the Great Court Cards. The Twos and Threes were found secretly taking the places specially resented for the Fours and Fives. Confusion had never been so confounded before.

Many spring seasons had come and gone in that Island of Cards. The Kokil, the bird of Spring, had sung its song year after year. But it had never stirred the blood as it stirred it now. In days gone by the sea had sung its tireless melody. But, then, it had proclaimed only the inflexible monotony of the Rule. And suddenly its waves were telling, through all their flashing light and luminous shade and myriad voices, the deepest yearnings of the heart of love!

VI

Where are vanished now their prim, round, regular, complacent features? Here is a face full of love-sick longing. Here is a heart heating wild with regrets. Here is a mind racked sore with doubts. Music and sighing, and smiles and tears, are filling the air. Life is throbbing; hearts are breaking; passions are kindling.

Everyone is now thinking of his own appearance, and comparing himself with others. The Ace of Clubs is musing to himself, that the King of Spades may be just passably good-looking. "But," says he, "when I walk down the street you have only to see how people's eyes turn towards me." The King of Spades is saying; "Why on earth is that Ace of Clubs always straining his neck and strutting about like a peacock? He imagines all the Queens are dying of love for him, while the real fact is "Here he pauses, and examines his face in the glass.

But the Queens were the worst of all. They began to spend all their time in dressing themselves up to the Nines. And the Nines would become their hopeless and abject slaves. But their cutting remarks about one another were more shocking still.

So the young men would sit listless on the leaves under the trees, lolling with outstretched limbs in the forest shade. And the young maidens, dressed in pale-blue robes, would come walking accidentally to the same shade of the same forest by the same trees, and turn their eyes as though they saw no one there, and look as though they came out to see nothing at all. And then one young man more forward than the rest in a fit of madness would dare to go near to a maiden in blue. But, as he drew near, speech would forsake him. He would stand there tongue-tied and foolish, and the favourable moment would pass.

The Kokil birds were singing in the boughs overhead. The mischievous South wind was blowing; it disarrayed the hair, it whispered in the ear, and stirred the music in the blood. The leaves of the trees were murmuring with rustling delight. And the ceaseless sound of the ocean made all the mute longings of the heart of man and maid surge backwards and forwards on the full springtide of love.

The Three Companions had brought into the dried-up channels of the Kingdom of Cards the full flood-tide of a new life.

VII

And, though the tide was full, there -was a pause as though the rising waters would not break into foam but remain suspended for ever. There were no outspoken words, only a cautious going forward one step and receding two. All seemed busy heaping up their unfulfilled desires like castles in the air, or fortresses of sand. They were pale and speechless, their eyes were burning, their lips trembling with unspoken secrets.

The Prince saw what was wrong. He summoned everyone on the Island and said: "Bring hither the flutes and the cymbals, the pipes and drums. Let all be played together, and raise loud shouts of rejoicing. For the Queen of Hearts this very night is going to choose her Mate !"

So the Tens and Nines began to blow on their flutes and pipes; the Eights and Sevens played on their sackbuts and viols; and even the Twos and Threes began to beat madly on their drums.

When this tumultuous gust of music came, it swept away at one blast all those sighings and mopings. And then what a torrent of laughter and words poured forth! There were daring proposals and locking refusals, and gossip and chatter, and jests and merriment. It was like the swaying and shaking, and rustling and soughing, in a summer gale, of a million leaves and branches in the depth of the primeval forest.

But the Queen of Hearts, in a rose-red robe, sat silent in the shadow of her secret bower, and listened to the great uproarious sound of music and mirth, that came floating towards her. She shut her eyes, and dreamt her dream of lore. And when she opened them she found the Prince seated on the ground before her gazing up at her face. And she covered her eyes with both hands, and shrank back quivering with an inward tumult of joy.

And the Prince passed the whole day alone, walking by the side of the surging sea. He carried in his mind that startled look, that shrinking gesture of the Queen, and his heart beat high with hope.

That night the serried, gaily-dressed ranks of young men and maidens waited with smiling faces at the Palace Gates. The Palace Hall was lighted with fairy lamps and festooned with the flowers of spring. Slowly the Queen of Hearts entered, and the whole assembly rose to greet her. With a jasmine garland in her hand, she stood before the Prince with downcast eyes. In her lowly bashfulness she could hardly raise the garland to the neck of the Mate she had chosen. But the Prince bowed his head, and the garland slipped to its place. The assembly of youths and maidens had waited her choice with eager, expectant hush. And when the choice was made, the whole vast concourse rocked and swayed with a tumult of wild delight. And the sound of their shouts was heard in every part of the island, and by ships far out at sea. Never had such a shout been raised in the Kingdom of Cards before.

And they carried the Prince and his Bride, and seated them on the throne, and crowned them then and there in the Ancient Island of Cards.

And the sorrowing Mother Queen, on the 'far-off island shore on the other side of the sea, came sailing to her son's new kingdom in a ship adorned with gold.

And the citizens are no longer regulated according to the Rules, but are good or bad, or both, according to their Ichcha.

The Renunciation

I

It was a night of full moon early in the month of Phalgun. The youthful spring was everywhere sending forth its breeze laden with the fragrance of mango-blossoms. The melodious notes of an untiring papiya (One of the sweetest songsters in Bengal. Anglo-Indian writers have nicknamed it the "brain-fever bird," which is a sheer libel.), concealed within the thick foliage of an old lichi tree by the side of a tank, penetrated a sleepless bedroom of the Mukerji family. There Hemanta now restlessly twisted a lock of his wife's hair round his finger, now beat her churl against her wristlet until it tinkled, now pulled at the chaplet of flowers about her head, and left it hanging over hex face. His mood was that of as evening breeze which played about a favourite flowering shrub, gently shaking her now this side, now that, in the hope of rousing her to animation.

But Kusum sat motionless, looking out of the open window, with eyes immersed in the moonlit depth of never-ending space beyond. Her husband's caresses were lost on her.

At last Hemanta clasped both the hands of his wife, and, shaking them gently, said: "Kusum, where are you? A patient search through a big telescope would reveal you only as a small speck-you seem to have receded so far away. O, do come closer to me, dear. See how beautiful the night is."

Kusum turned her eyes from the void of space towards her husband, and said slowly: "I know a mantra (A set of magic words.), which could in one moment shatter this spring night and the moon into pieces."

"If you do," laughed Hemanta, "pray don't utter it. If any mantra of yours could bring three or four Saturdays during the week, and prolong the nights till 5 P.M. the next day, say it by all means."

Saying this, he tried to draw his wife a little closer to him. Kusum, freeing herself from the embrace, said: "Do you know, to-night I feel a longing to tell you what I promised to reveal only on my death-bed. To-night I feel that I could endure whatever punishment you might inflict on me."

Hemanta was on the point of making a jest about punishments by reciting a verse from Jayadeva, when the sound of an angry pair of slippers was heard approaching rapidly. They were the familiar footsteps of his father, Haribar Mukerji, and Hemanta, not knowing what it meant, was in a flutter of excitement.

Standing outside the door Harihar roared out: "Hemanta, turn your wife out of the house immediately."

Hemanta looked at his wife, and detected no trace of surprise in her features. She merely buried her face within the palms of her hands, and, with all the strength and intensity of her soul, wished that she could then and there melt into nothingness. It was the same papiya whose song floated into the room with the south breeze, and no one heard it. Endless are the beauties of the earth-but alas, how easily everything is twisted out of shape.

II

Returning from without, Hemanta asked his wife: "Is it true?"

"It is," replied Kusum.

"Why didn't you tell me long ago?"

"I did try many a time, and I always failed. I am a wretched woman."

"Then tell me everything now."

Kusum gravely told her story in a firm unshaken voice. She waded barefooted through fire, as it were, with slow unflinching steps, and nobody knew how much she was scorched. Having heard her to the end, Hemanta rose and walked out.

Kusum thought that her husband had gone, never to return to her again. It did not strike her as strange. She took it as naturally as any other incident of everyday life-so dry and apathetic had her mind become during the last few moments. Only the world and love seemed to her as a void and make-believe from beginning to end. Even the memory of the protestations of love, which her husband had made to her in days past, brought to her lips a dry, hard, joyless smile, like a sharp cruel knife which had cut through her heart. She was thinking, perhaps, that the love which seemed to fill so much of one's life, which brought in its train such fondness and depth of feeling, which made even the briefest separation so exquisitely painful and a moment's union so intensely sweet, which seemed boundless in its extent and eternal in its duration, the cessation of which could not be imagined even in births to come, that this was that love! So feeble was its support! No sooner does the priesthood touch it than your "eternal" love crumbles into a handful of dust! Only a short while ago Hemanta had whispered to her: "What a beautiful night!" The same night was not yet at an end, the same yapiya was still warbling, the same south breeze still blew into the roam, making the bed-curtain shiver; the same moonlight lay on the bed next the open window, sleeping like a beautiful heroine exhausted with gaiety. All this was unreal! Love was more falsely dissembling than she herself!

III

The next morning Hemanta, fagged after a sleepless night, and looking like one distracted, called at the house of Peari Sankar Ghosal. "What news, my son?" Peari Sankar greeted him.

Hemanta, flaring up like a big fire, said in a trembling voice: "You have defiled our caste. You have brought destruction upon us. And you will have to pay for it." He could say no more; be felt choked.

"And you have preserved my caste, presented my ostracism from the community, and patted me on the back affectionately!" said Peari Sankar with a slight sarcastic smile.

Hemanta wished that his Brahmin-fury could reduce Peari Sankar to ashes in a moment, but his rage burnt only himself. Peari Sankar sat before him unscathed, and in the best of health.

"Did I ever do you any harm?" demanded Hemanta in a broken voice.

"Let me ask you one question," said Peari Sankar. "My daughter, my only child—what harm had she done your father? You were very young then, and probably never heard. Listen, then. Now, don't you excite yourself. There is much humour in what I am going to relate.

"You were quite small when my son-in-law Nabakanta ran away to England after stealing my daughter's jewels. You might truly remember the commotion in the village when he returned as a barrister five years later. Or, perhaps, you were unaware of it, as you were at school in Calcutta at the time. Your father, arrogating to himself the headship of the community, declared that if I sent my daughter to her husband's home, I must renounce her for good, and never again allow her to cross my threshold. I fell at your father's feet, and implored him, saying: 'Brother, save me this once. I will make the boy swallow cow-dung, and go through the prayaschittam ceremony. Do take him back into caste.' But your father remained obdurate. For my part, I could not disown my only child, and, bidding good-bye to my village and my kinsmen, I betook myself to Calcutta. There, too, my troubles followed me. When I had made every arrangement for my nephew's marriage, your father stirred up the girl's people, and they broke the match off. Then I took a solemn vow that, if there was a drop of Brahmin blood flowing in my veins, I would avenge myself. You understand the business to some extent now, don't you? But wait a little longer. You will enjoy it, when I tell you the whole story; it is interesting.

"When you were attending college, one Bipradas Chatterji used to live next door to your lodgings. The poor fellow is dead now. In his house lived a child-widow called Kusum, the destitute orphan of a Kayestha gentleman. The girl was very pretty, and the old Brahmin desired to shield her from the hungry gaze of college students. But for a young girl to throw dust in the eyes of her old guardian was not at all a difficult task. She often went to the top of the roof, to hang her washing out to dry, and, I believe, you found your own roof best suited for your studies. Whether you two spoke to each other, when on your respective roofs, I cannot tell, but the girl's behaviour excited suspicion in the old man's mind. She made frequent mistakes in her household duties, and, like Parbati (The wife of Shiva the Destroyer), engaged in her devotions, began gradually to renounce food and sleep. Some evenings she would burst into tears in the presence of the old gentleman, without any apparent reason.

"At last he discovered that you two saw each other from the roofs pretty frequently, and that you even went the length of absenting yourself from college to sit on the roof at mid-day with a book in your hand, so fond had you grown suddenly of solitary study. Bipradas came to me for advice, and told me everything. 'Uncle,' said I to him, `for a long while you have cherished a desire to go on a pilgrimage to Benares. You had better do it now, and leave the girl in my charge. I will take care of her.'

"So he went. I lodged the girl in the house of Sripati Chatterji, passing him off as her father. What happened next is known to you. I feel a great relief to-day, having told you everything from the beginning. It sounds like a romance, doesn't it? I think of turning it into a book, and getting it printed. But I am not a writing-man myself. They say my nephew has some aptitude that way, I will get him to write it for me. But the best thing would be, if you would collaborate with him, because the conclusion of the story is not known to me so well."

Without paying much attention to the concluding remarks of Peari Sankar, Hemanta asked: "Did not Kusum object to this marriage?"

"Well," said Peari Sankar, "it is very difficult to guess. You know, my boy, how women's minds are constituted. When they say 'no,' they mean 'yes.' During the first few days after her removal to the new home, she went almost crazy at not seeing you. You, too, seemed to have discovered her new address somehow, as you used to lose your way after starting for college, and loiter about in front of Sripati's house. Your eyes did not appear to be exactly in search of the Presidency College, as they were directed towards the barred windows of a private house, through which nothing but insects and the hearts of moon-struck young men could obtain access. I felt very sorry for you both. I could see that your studies were being seriously interrupted, and that the plight of the girl was pitiable also.

"One day I called Kusum to me, and said: 'Listen to me, my daughter. I am an old man, and you need feel no delicacy in my presence. I know whom you desire at heart. The young man's condition is hopeless too. I wish I could bring about your union.' At this Kusum suddenly melted into tears, and ran away. On several evenings after that, I visited Sripati's house, and, calling Kusum to me, discussed with her matters relating to you, and so I succeeded in gradually overcoming her shyness. At last, when I said that I would try to bring about a marriage, she asked me: 'How can it be?' 'Never mind,' I said, 'I would pass you off as a Brahmin maiden.' After a good deal of argument, she begged me to find out whether you would approve of it. 'What nonsense,' replied I, 'the boy is well-nigh mad as it were, what's the use of disclosing all these complications to him? Let the ceremony be over smoothly and then, all's well that ends well. Especially, as there is not the slightest risk of its ever leaking out, why go out of the way to make a fellow miserable for life?'

"I do not know whether the plan had Kusum's assent or not. At times she wept, and at other times she remained silent. If I said, `Let us drop it then,' she would become very restless. When things were in this state, I sent Sripati to you with the proposal of marriage; you consented without a moment's hesitation. Everything was settled.

"Shortly before the day fixed, Kusum became so obstinate that I had the greatest difficulty in bringing her round again. `Do let it drop, uncle,' she said to me constantly. 'What do you mean, you silly child,' I rebuked her,' how can we back out now, when everything has been settled?'

"'Spread a rumour that I am dead,' she implored. 'Send me away somewhere.'

"'What would happen to the young man then?' said I.' He is now in the seventh heaven of delight, expecting that his long cherished desire would be fulfilled to-morrow; and to-day you want me to send him the news of your death. The result would be that to-morrow I should have to bear the news of his death to you, and the same evening your death would be reported to me. Do you imagine, child, that I am capable of committing a girl-murder and a Brahmin-murder at my age?'

"Eventually the happy marriage was celebrated at the auspicious moment, and I felt relieved of a burdensome duty which I owed to myself. What happened afterwards you know best."

"Couldn't you stop after having done us an irreparable injury?" burst out Hemanta after a short silence. "Why have you told the secret now?"

With the utmost composure, Peari Sankar replied: "When I saw that all arrangements had been made for the wedding of your sister, I said to myself: 'Well, I have fouled the caste of one Brahmin, but that was only from a sense of duty. Here, another Brahmin's caste is imperilled, and this time it is my plain duty to prevent it.' So I wrote to them saying that I was in a position to prove that you bad taken the daughter of a sudra to wife."

Controlling himself with a gigantic effort, Hemanta said: "What will become of this girl whom I shall abandon now? Would you give her food and shelter?"

"I have done what was mine to do," replied Peari Sankar calmly. "It is no part of my duty to look after the discarded wives of other people. Anybody there? Get a glass of cocoanut milk for Hemanta Babu with ice in it. And some pan too."

Hemanta rose, and took his departure without waiting for this luxurious hospitality.

IV

It was the fifth night of the waning of the moon and the night was dark. No birds were singing. The lichi tree by the tank looked like a smudge of ink on a background a shade less deep. The south wind was blindly roaming about in the darkness like a sleep-walker. The stars in the sky with vigilant unblinking eyes were trying to penetrate the darkness, in their effort to fathom some profound mystery.

No light shone in the bedroom. Hemanta was sitting on the side of the bed next the open window, gazing at the darkness in front of him. Kusum lay on the floor, clasping her husband's feet with both her arms, and her face resting on them. Time stood like an ocean hushed into stillness. On the background of eternal night, Fate seemed to have painted this one single picture for all time annihilation on every side, the judge in the centre of it, and the guilty one at his feet.

The sound of slippers was heard again. Approaching the door, Harihar Mukerji said: "You have had enough time, I can't allow you more. Turn the girl out of the house."

Kusum, as she heard this, embraced her husband's feet with all the ardour of a lifetime, covered them with kisses, and touching her forehead to them reverentially, withdrew herself.

Hemanta rose, and walking to the door, said: "Father, I won't forsake my wife."

"What!" roared out Harihar, "would you lose your caste, sir?"

"I don't care for caste," was Hemanta's calm reply.

"Then you too I renounce."

Vision

I

When I was a very young wife, I gave birth to a dead child, and came near to death myself. I recovered strength very slowly, and my eyesight became weaker and weaker.

My husband at this time was studying medicine. He was not altogether sorry to have a chance of testing his medical knowledge on me. So he began to treat my eyes himself.

My elder brother was reading for his law examination. One day he came to see me, and was alarmed at my condition.

"What are you doing?" he said to my husband. "You are ruining Kumo's eyes. You ought to consult a good doctor at once."

My husband said irritably: "Why! what can a good doctor do more than I am doing? The case is quite a simple one, and the remedies are all well known."

Dada answered with scorn: "I suppose you think there is no difference between you and a Professor in your own Medical College."

My husband replied angrily: "If you ever get married, and there is a dispute about your wife's property, you won't take my advice about Law. Why, then, do you now come advising me about Medicine?"

While they were quarrelling, I was saying to myself that it was always the poor grass that suffered most when two kings went to war. Here was a dispute going on between these two, and I had to bear the brunt of it.

It also seemed to me very unfair that, when my family had given me in marriage, they should interfere afterwards. After all, my pleasure and pain are my husband's concern, not theirs.

From that day forward, merely over this trifling matter of my eyes, the bond between my husband and Dada was strained.

To my surprise one afternoon, while my husband was away, Dada brought a doctor in to see me. He examined my eyes very carefully, and looked grave. He said that further neglect would be dangerous. He wrote out a prescription, and Dada for the medicine at once. When the strange doctor had gone, I implored my Dada not to interfere. I was sure that only evil would come from the stealthy visits of a doctor.

I was surprised at myself for plucking up courage speak to my brother like that. I had always hitherto been afraid of him. I am sure also that Dada was surprised at my boldness. He kept silence for a while, and then said to me: "Very well, Kumo. I won't call in the doctor any more. But when the medicine comes you must take it."

Dada then went away. The medicine came from chemist. I took it, bottles, powders, prescriptions and all, and threw it down the well!

My husband had been irritated by Dada's interference, and he began to treat my eyes with greater diligence than ever. He tried all sorts of remedies. I bandaged my eyes as he told me, I wore his coloured glasses, I put in his drops, I took all his powders. I even drank the cod-liver oil he gave me, though my gorge rose against it.

Each time he came back from the hospital, he would ask me anxiously how I felt; and I would answer: "Oh! much better." Indeed I became an expert in self-delusion. When I found that the water in my eyes was still increasing, I would console myself with the thought that it was a good thing to get rid of so much bad fluid; and, when the flow of water in my eyes decreased, I was elated at my husband's skill.

But after a while the agony became unbearable. My eyesight faded away, and I had continual headaches day and night. I saw how much alarmed my husband was getting. I gathered from his manner that he was casting about for a pretext to call in a doctor. So I hinted that it might be as well to call one in.

That he was greatly relieved, I could see. He called in an English doctor that very day. I do not know what talk they had together, but I gathered that the Sahib had spoken very sharply to my husband.

He remained silent for some time after the doctor had gone. I took his hands in mine, and said: "What an ill-mannered brute that was! Why didn't you call in an Indian doctor? That would have been much better. Do you think that man knows better than you do about my eyes?"

My husband was very silent for a moment, and then said with a broken voice: "Kumo, your eyes must be operated on."

I pretended to be vexed with him for concealing the fact from me so long.

"Here you have known this all the time," said I, "and yet you have said nothing about it! Do you think I am such a baby as to be afraid of an operation?"

At that be regained his good spirits: "There are very few men," said he, "who are heroic enough to look forward to an operation without shrinking."

I laughed at him: "Yes, that is so. Men are heroic only before their wives!"

He looked at me gravely, and said: "You are perfectly right. We men are dreadfully vain."

I laughed away his seriousness: "Are you sure you can beat us women even in vanity? "

When Dada came, I took him aside: "Dada, that treatment your doctor recommended would have done me a world of good; only unfortunately. I mistook the mixture for the lotion. And since the day I made the mistake, my eyes have grown steadily worse; and now an operation is needed."

Dada said to me: "You were under your husband's treatment, and that is why I gave up coming to visit you."

"No," I answered. "In reality, I was secretly treating myself in accordance with your doctor's directions."

Oh! what lies we women have to tell! When we are mothers, we tell lies to pacify our children; and when we are wives, we tell lies to pacify the fathers of our children. We are never free from this necessity.

My deception had the effect of bringing about a better feeling between my husband and Dada. Dada blamed himself for asking me to keep a secret from my husband: and my husband regretted that he had not taken my brother's advice at the first.

At last, with the consent of both, an English doctor came, and operated on my left eye. That eye, however, was too weak to bear the strain; and the last flickering glimmer of light went out. Then the other eye gradually lost itself in darkness.

One day my husband came to my bedside. "I cannot brazen it out before you any longer," said he, "Kumo, it is I who have ruined your eyes."

I felt that his voice was choking with tears, and so I took up his right hand in both of mine and said: "Why! you did exactly what was right. You have dealt only with that which was your very own. Just imagine, if some strange doctor had come and taken away my eyesight. What consolation should I have had then? But now I can feel that all has happened for the best; and my great comfort is to know that it is at your hands I have lost my eyes. When Ramchandra found one lotus too few with which to worship God, he offered both his eyes in place of the lotus. And I hate dedicated my eyes to my God. From now, whenever you see something that is a joy to you, then you must describe it to me; and I will feed upon your words as a sacred gift left over from your vision."

I do not mean, of course, that I said all this there and then, for it is impossible to speak these things an the spur of the moment. But I used to think over words like these for days and days together. And when I was very depressed, or if at any time the light of my devotion became dim, and I pitied my evil fate, then I made my mind utter these sentences, one by one, as a child repeats a story that is told. And so I could breathe once more the serener air of peace and love.

At the very time of our talk together, I said enough to show my husband what was in my heart.

"Kumo," he said to me, "the mischief I have done by my folly can never be made good. But I can do one thing. I can ever remain by your side, and try to make up for your want of vision as much as is in my power."

"No," said I. "That will never do. I shall not ask you to turn your house into an hospital for the blind. There is only one thing to be done, you must marry again."

As I tried to explain to him that this was necessary, my voice broke a little. I coughed, and tried to hide my emotion, but he burst out saying:

"Kumo, I know I am a fool, and a braggart, and all that, but I am not a villain! If ever I marry again, I swear to you, I swear to you the most solemn oath by my family god, Gopinath may that most hated of all sins, the sin of parricide, fall on my head!"

Ah! I should never, never have allowed him to swear that dreadful oath. But tears were choking my voice, and I could not say a word for insufferable joy. I hid my blind face in my pillows, and sobbed, and sobbed again. At last, when the first flood of my tears was over, I drew his head down to my breast.

"Ah I" said I, "why did you take such a terrible oath? Do you think I asked you to marry again for your own sordid pleasure? No! I was thinking of myself, for she could perform those services which were mine to give you when I had my sight."

"Services!" said he, "services! Those can be done by servants. Do you think I am mad enough to bring a slave into my house, and bid her share the throne with this my Goddess?"

As he said the word "Goddess," he held up my face in his hands, and placed a kiss between my brows. At that moment the third eye of divine wisdom was opened, where he kissed me, and verily I had a consecration.

I said in my own mind: "It is well. I am no longer able to serve him in the lower world of household cares. But I shall rise to a higher region. I shall bring down blessings from above. No more lies! No more deceptions for me! All the littlenesses and hypocrisies of my former life shall be banished forever!"

That day, the whole day through, I felt a conflict going on within me. The joy of the thought, that after this solemn oath it was impossible for my husband to marry again, fixed its roots deep in my heart, and I could not tear them out. But the new Goddess, who had taken her new throne in me, said: "The time might come when it would be good for your husband to break his oath and marry again." But the woman, who was within me, said: "That may be; but all the same an oath is an oath, and there is no way out." The Goddess, who was within me, answered: "That is no reason why you should exult over it." But the woman, who was within me, replied: "What you say is quite true, no doubt; all the same he has taken his oath." And the same story went on again and again. At last the Goddess frowned in silence, and the darkness of a horrible fear came down upon me.

My repentant husband would not let the servants do my work; he must do it all himself. At first it gave me unbounded delight to be dependent on him thus for every little thing. It was a means of keeping him by my side, and my desire to have him with me had become intense since my blindness. That share of his presence, which my eyes had lost, my other senses craved. When he was absent from my side, I would feel as if I were hanging in mid-air, and had lost my hold of all things tangible.

Formerly, when my husband came back late from the hospital, I used to open my window and gaze at the road. That road was the link which connected his world with mine. Now when I had lost that link through my blindness, all my body would go out to seek him. The bridge that united us had given way, and there was now this unsurpassable chasm. When he left my side the gulf seemed to yawn wide open. I could only wait for the time when he should cross back again from his own shore to mine.

But such intense longing and such utter dependence can never be good. A wife is a burden enough to a man, in all conscience, and to add to it the burden of this blindness was to make his life unbearable. I vowed that I would suffer alone, and never wrap my husband round in the folds of my all-pervading darkness.

Within an incredibly short space of time I managed to train myself to do all my household duties by the help of touch and sound and smell. In fact I soon found that I could get on with greater skill than before. For sight often distracts rather than helps us. And so it came to pass that, when these roving eyes of mine could do their work no longer, all the other senses took up their several duties with quietude and completeness.

When I had gained experience by constant practice, I would not let my husband do any more household duties for me. He complained bitterly at first that I was depriving him of his penance.

This did not convince me. Whatever he might say, I could feel that he had a real sense of relief when these household duties were over. To serve daily a wife who is blind can never make up the life of a man.

II

My husband at last had finished his medical course. He went away from Calcutta to a small town to practise as a doctor. There in the country I felt with joy, through all my blindness, that I was restored to the arms of my mother. I had left my village birthplace for Calcutta when I was eight years old. Since then ten years had passed away, and in the great city the memory of my village home had grown dim. As long as I had eyesight, Calcutta with its busy life screened from view the memory of my early days. But when I lost my eyesight I knew for the first time that Calcutta allured only the eyes: it could not fill the mind. And now, in my blindness, the scenes of my childhood shone out once more, like stars that appear one by one in the evening sky at the end of the day.

It was the beginning of November when we left Calcutta for Harsingpur. The place was new to me, but the scents and sounds of the countryside pressed round and embraced me. The morning breeze coming fresh from the newly ploughed land, the sweet and tender smell of the flowering mustard, the shepherd-boy's flute sounding in the distance, even the creaking noise of the bullock-cart, as it groaned over the broken village road, filled my world with delight. The memory of my past life, with all its ineffable fragrance and sound, became a living present to me, and my blind eyes could not tell me I was wrong. I went back, and lived over again my childhood. Only one thing was absent: my mother was not with me.

I could see my home with the large peepul trees growing along the edge of the village pool. I could picture in my mind's eye my old grandmother seated on the ground with her thin wisps of hair untied, warming her back in the sun as she made the little round lentil balls to be dried and used for cooking. But somehow I could not recall the songs she used to croon to herself in her weak and quavering voice. In the evening, whenever I heard the lowing of cattle, I could almost watch the figure of my mother going round the sheds with lighted lamp in her hand. The smell of the wet fodder and the pungent smoke of the straw fire would enter into my very heart. And in the distance I seemed to hear the clanging of the temple bell wafted up by the breeze from the river bank.

Calcutta, with all its turmoil and gossip, curdles the heart. There, all the beautiful duties of life lose their freshness and innocence. I remember one day, when a friend of mine came in, and said to me: "Kumo, why don't you feel angry? If I had been treated like you by my husband, I would never look upon his face again."

She tried to make me indignant, because he had been so long calling in a doctor.

"My blindness," said I, "was itself a sufficient evil. Why should I make it worse by allowing hatred to grow up against my husband?"

My friend shook her head in great contempt, when she heard such old-fashioned talk from the lips of a mere chit of a girl. She went away in disdain. But whatever might be my answer at the time, such words as these left their poison; and the venom was never wholly got out of the soul, when once they had been uttered.

So you see Calcutta, with its never-ending gossip, does harden the heart. But when I came back to the country all my earlier hopes and faiths, all that I held true in life during childhood, became fresh and bright once more. God came to me, and filled my heart and my world. I bowed to Him, and said:

"It is well that Thou has taken away my eyes. Thou art with me."

Ah! But I said more than was right. It was a presumption to say: "Thou art with me." All we can say is this: "I must be true to Thee." Even when nothing is left for us, still we have to go on living.

III

We passed a few happy months together. My husband gained some reputation in his profession as a doctor. And money came with it.

But there is a mischief in money. I cannot point to any one event; but, because the blind have keener perceptions than other people, I could discern the change which came over my husband along with the increase of wealth.

He had a keen sense of justice when he was younger, and had often told me of his great desire to help the poor when once he obtained a practice of his own. He had a noble contempt far those in his profession who would not feel the pulse of a poor patient before collecting his fee. But now I noticed a difference. He had become strangely hard. Once when a poor woman came, and begged him, out of charity, to save the life of her only child, he bluntly refused. And when I implored him myself to help her, he did his work perfunctorily.

While we were less rich my husband disliked sharp practice in money matters. He was scrupulously honourable in such things. But since he had got a large account at the bank he was often closeted for hours with some scamp of a landlord's agent, for purposes which clearly boded no good.

Where has he drifted? What has become of this husband of mine, the husband I knew before I was blind; the husband who kissed me that day between my brows, and enshrined me on the throne of a Goddess? Those whom a sudden gust of passion brings down to the dust can rise up again with a new strong impulse of goodness. But those who, day by day, become dried up in the very fibre of their moral being; those who by some outer parasitic growth choke the inner life by slow degrees, such wench one day a deadness which knows no healing.

The separation caused by blindness is the merest physical trifle. But, ah! it suffocates me to find that he is no longer with me, where he stood with me in that hour when we both knew that I was blind. That is a separation indeed!

I, with my love fresh and my faith unbroken, have kept to the shelter of my heart's inner shrine. But my husband has left the cool shade of those things that are ageless and unfading. He is fast disappearing into the barren, waterless waste in his mad thirst for gold.

Sometimes the suspicion comes to me that things not so bad as they seem: that perhaps I exaggerate because I am blind. It may be that, if my eyesight were unimpaired, I should have accepted world as I found it. This, at any rate, was the light in which my husband looked at all my moods and fancies.

One day an old Musalman came to the house. He asked my husband to visit his little grand-daughter. I could hear the old man say: "Baba, I am a poor man; but come with me, and Allah will do you good." My husband answered coldly: "What Allah will do won't help matters; I want to know what you can do for me."

When I heard it, I wondered in my mind why God had not made me deaf as well as blind. The old man heaved a deep sigh, and departed. I sent my maid to fetch him to my room. I met him at the door of the inner apartment, and put some money into his hand.

"Please take this from me," said I, "for your little grand-daughter, and get a trustworthy doctor to look after her. And-pray for my husband."

But the whole of that day I could take no food at all. In the afternoon, when my husband got up from sleep, he asked me: "Why do you look so pale?"

I was about to say, as I used to do in the past: "Oh! It's nothing "; but those days of deception were over, and I spoke to him plainly.

"I have been hesitating," I said, "for days together to tell you something. It has been hard to think out what exactly it was I wanted to say. Even now I may not be able to explain what I had in my mind. But I am sure you know what has happened. Our lives have drifted apart."

My husband laughed in a forced manner, and said: "Change is the law of nature."

I said to him: "I know that. But there are some things that are eternal."

Then he became serious.

"There are many women," said he, "who have a real cause for sorrow. There are some whose husbands do not earn money. There are others whose husbands do not love them. But you are making yourself wretched about nothing at all."

Then it became clear to me that my very blindness had conferred on me the power of seeing a world which is beyond all change. Yes! It is true. I am not like other women. And my husband will never understand me.

IV

Our two lives went on with their dull routine for some time. Then there was a break in the monotony. An aunt of my husband came to pay us a visit.

The first thing she blurted out after our first greeting was this: "Well, Krum, it's a great pity you have become blind; but why do you impose your own affliction on your husband? You must get him to another wife."

There was an awkward pause. If my husband had only said something in jest, or laughed in her face, all would have been over. But he stammered and hesitated, and said at last in a nervous, stupid way: "Do you really think so? Really, Aunt, you shouldn't talk like that"

His aunt appealed to me. "Was I wrong, Kumo?"

I laughed a hollow laugh.

"Had not you better," said I, "consult some one more competent to decide? The pickpocket never asks permission from the man whose pocket he is going to pick."

"You are quite right," she replied blandly. "Abinash, my dear, let us have our little conference in private. What do you say to that?"

After a few days my husband asked her, in my presence, if she knew of any girl of a decent family who could come and help me in my household work. He knew quite well that I needed no help. I kept silence.

"Oh! there are heaps of them," replied his aunt. "My cousin has a daughter who is just of the marriageable age, and as nice a girl as you could wish. Her people would be only too glad to secure you as a husband."

Again there came from him that forced, hesitating laugh, and he said: "But I never mentioned marriage."

"How could you expect," asked his aunt, "a girl of decent family to come and live in your house without marriage? "

He had to admit that this was reasonable, and remained nervously silent.

I stood alone within the closed doors of my blindness after he had gone, and called upon my God and prayed: "O God, save my husband."

When I was coming out of the household shrine from my morning worship a few days later, his aunt took hold of both my hands warmly.

"Kumo, here is the girl," said she, "we were speaking about the other day. Her name is Hemangini. She will be delighted to meet you. Hemo, come here and be introduced to your sister."

My husband entered the room at the same moment. He feigned surprise when he saw the strange girl, and was about to retire. But his aunt said: "Abinash, my dear, what are you running away for? There is no need to do that. Here is my cousin's daughter, Hemangini, come to see you. Hemo, make your bow to him."

As if taken quite by surprise, he began to ply his aunt with questions about the when and why and how of the new arrival.

I saw the hollowness of the whole thing, and took Hemangini by the hand and led her to my own room. I gently stroked her face and arms and hair, and found that she was about fifteen years old, and very beautiful.

As I felt her face, she suddenly burst out laughing and said: "Why! what are you doing? Are you hypnotising me?"

That sweet ringing laughter of hers swept away in a moment all the dark clouds that stood between us. I threw my right arm about her neck.

"Dear one," said I, "I am trying to see you." And again I stroked her soft face with my left hand.

"Trying to see me?" she said, with a new burst of laughter. "Am I like a vegetable marrow, grown in your garden, that you want to feel me all round to see how soft I am?"

I suddenly bethought me that she did not know I had lost my sight.

"Sister, I am blind," said I.

She was silent. I could feel her big young eyes, full of curiosity, peering into my face. I knew they were full of pity. Then she grew thoughtful and puzzled, and said, after a short pause:

"Oh! I see now. That was the reason your husband invited his aunt to come and stay here."

"No!" I replied, "you are quite mistaken. He did not ask her to come. She came of her own accord."

Hemangini went off into a peal of laughter. "That's just like my aunt," said she. "Oh I wasn't it nice of her to come without any invitation? But now she's come, you won't get her to move for some time, I can assure you!"

Then she paused, and looked puzzled.

"But why did father send me?" she asked. "Can you tell me that? "

The aunt had come into the room while we were talking. Hemangini said to her: "When are you thinking of going back, Aunt? "

The aunt looked very much upset.

"What a question to ask!" said she, "I've never seen such a restless body as you. We've only just come, and you ask when we're going back!"

"It is all very well for you," Hemangini said, "for this house belongs to your near relations. But what about me? I tell you plainly I can't stop here." And then she held my hand and said: "What do you think, dear?"

I drew her to my heart, but said nothing. The aunt was in a great difficulty. She felt the situation was getting beyond her control; so she proposed that she and her niece should go out together to bathe.

"No! we two will go together," said Hemangini, clinging to me. The aunt gave in, fearing opposition if she tried to drag her away.

Going down to the river Hemangini asked me: "Why don't you have children? "

I was startled by her question, and answered: "How can I tell? My God has not given me any. That is the reason."

"No! That's not the reason," said Hemangini quickly. "You must have committed some sin. Look at my aunt. She is childless. It must be because her heart has some wickedness. But what wickedness is in your heart?"

The words hurt me. I have no solution to offer for the problem of evil. I sighed deeply, and said in the silence of my soul: "My God! Thou knowest the reason."

"Gracious goodness," cried Hemangini, "what are you sighing for? No one ever takes me seriously."

And her laughter pealed across the river.

V

I found out after this that there were constant interruptions in my husband's professional duties. He refused all calls from a distance, and would hurry away from his patients, even when they were close at hand.

Formerly it was only during the mid-day meals and at night-time that he could come into the inner apartment. But now, with unnecessary anxiety for his aunt's comfort, he began to visit her at all hours of the day. I knew at once that he had come to her room, when I heard her shouting for Hemangini to bring in a glass of water. At first the girl would do what she was told; but later on she refused altogether.

Then the aunt would call, in an endearing voice: "Hemo! Hemo! Hemangini." But the girl would cling to me with an impulse of pity. A sense of dread and sadness would keep her silent. Sometimes she would shrink towards me like a hunted thing, who scarcely knew what was coming.

About this time my brother came down from Calcutta to visit me. I knew how keen his powers of observation were, and what a hard judge he was. I feared my husband would be put on his defence, and have to stand his trial before him. So I endeavoured to hide the true situation behind a mask of noisy cheerfulness. But I am afraid I overdid the part: it was unnatural for me.

My husband began to fidget openly, and asked bow long my brother was going to stay. At last his impatience became little short of insulting, and my brother had no help for it but to leave. Before going he placed his hand on my head, and kept it there for some time. I noticed that his hand shook, and a tear fell from his eyes, as he silently gave me his blessing.

I well remember that it was an evening in April, and a market-day. People who had come into the town were going back home from market. There was the feeling of an impending storm in the air; the smell of the wet earth and the moisture in the wind were all-pervading. I never keep a lighted lamp in my bedroom, when I am alone, lest my clothes should catch fire, or some accident happen. I sat on the floor in my dark room, and called upon the God of my blind world.

"O my Lord," I cried, "Thy face is hidden. I cannot see. I am blind. I hold tight this broken rudder of a heart till my hands bleed. The waves have become too strong for me. How long wilt thou try me, my God, how long?"

I kept my head prone upon the bedstead and began to sob. As I did so, I felt the bedstead move a little. The next moment Hemangini was by my side. She clung to my neck, and wiped my tears away silently. I do not know why she had been waiting that evening in the inner room, or why she had been lying alone there in the dusk. She asked me no question. She said no word. She simply placed her cool hand on my forehead, and kissed me, and departed.

The next morning Hemangini said to her aunt in my presence : "If you want to stay on, you can. But I don't. I'm going away home with our family servant."

The aunt said there was no need for her to go alone, for she was going away also. Then smilingly and mincingly she brought out, from a plush case, a ring set with pearls.

"Look, Hemo," said she, "what a beautiful ring my Abinash brought for you."

Hemangini snatched the ring from her hand.

"Look, Aunt," she answered quickly, "just see how splendidly I aim." And she flung the ring into the tank outside the window.

The aunt, overwhelmed with alarm, vexation, and surprise, bristled like a hedgehog. She turned to me, and held me by the hand.

"Kumo," she repeated again and again, "don't say a word about this childish freak to Abinash. He would be fearfully vexed."

I assured her that she need not fear. Not a word would reach him about it from my lips.

The next day before starting for home Hemangini embraced me, and said: "Dearest, keep me in mind; do not forget me."

I stroked her face over and over with my fingers, and said: "Sister, the blind have long memories."

I drew her head towards me, and kissed her hair and her forehead. My world suddenly became grey. All the beauty and laughter and tender youth, which had nestled so close to me, vanished when Hemangini departed. I went groping about with arms outstretched, seeking to find out what was left in my deserted world.

My husband came in later. He affected a great relief now that they were gone, but it was exaggerated and empty. He pretended that his aunt's visit had kept him away from work.

Hitherto there had been only the one barrier of blindness between me and my husband. Now another barrier was added, this deliberate silence about Hemangini. He feigned utter indifference, but I knew he was having letters about her.

It was early in May. My maid entered my room one morning, and asked me: "What is all this preparation going on at the landing on the river? Where is Master going?"

I knew there was something impending, but I said to the maid: "I can't say."

The maid did not dare to ask me any more questions. She sighed, and went away.

Late that night my husband came to me.

"I have to visit a patient in the country," said he. "I shall have to start very early to-morrow morning, and I may have to be away for two or three days."

I got up from my bed. I stood before him, and cried aloud: "Why are you telling me lies?"

My husband stammered out: "What - what lies have I told you?"

I said: "You are going to get married."

He remained silent. For some moments there was no sound in the room. Then I broke the silence:

"Answer me," I cried. "Say, yes."

He answered, "Yes," like a feeble echo.

I shouted out with a loud voice: "No! I shall never allow you. I shall save you from this great disaster, this dreadful sin. If I fail in this, then why am I your wife, and why did I ever worship my God?"

The room remained still as a stone. I dropped on the floor, and clung to my husband's knees.

"What have I done?" I asked. "Where have I been lacking? Tell me truly. Why do you want another wife?"

My husband said slowly: "I will tell you the truth. I am afraid of you. Your blindness has enclosed you in its fortress, and I have now no entrance. To me you are no longer a woman. You are awful as my God. I cannot live my everyday life with you. I want a woman, just an ordinary woman, whom I can be free to chide and coax and pet and scold."

Oh, tear open my heart and see! What am I else but that, just an ordinary woman? I am the same girl that I was when I was newlywed, a girl with all her need to believe, to confide, to worship.

I do not recollect exactly the words that I uttered. I only remember that I said: "If I be a true wife, then, may God be my witness, you shall never do this wicked deed, you shall never break your oath. Before you commit such sacrilege, either I shall become a widow, or Hemangini shall die."

Then I fell down on the floor in a swoon. When I came to myself, it was still dark. The birds were silent. My husband had gone.

All that day I sat at my worship in the sanctuary at the household shrine. In the evening a fierce storm, with thunder and lightning and rain, swept down upon the house and shook it. As I crouched before the shrine, I did not ask my God to save my husband from the storm, though he must have been at that time in peril on the river. I prayed that whatever might happen to me, my husband might be saved from this great sin.

Night passed. The whole of the next day I kept my seat at worship. When it was evening there was the noise of shaking and beating at the door. When the door was broken open, they found me lying unconscious on the ground, and carried me to my room.

When I came to myself at last, I heard someone whispering in my ear: "Sister."

I found that I was lying in my room with my head on Hemangini's lap. When my head moved, I heard her dress rustle. It was the sound of bridal silk.

O my God, my God! My prayer has gone unheeded! My husband has fallen!

Hemangini bent her head low, and said in a sweet whisper: "Sister, dearest, I have come to ask your blessing on our marriage."

At first my whole body stiffened like the trunk of a tree that has been struck by lightning. Then I sat up, and said, painfully, forcing myself to speak the words: "Why should I not bless you? You have done no wrong."

Hemangini laughed her merry laugh.

"Wrong!" said she. "When you married it was right; and when I marry, you call it wrong! "

I tried to smile in answer to her laughter. I said in my mind: "My prayer is not the final thing in this world. His will is all. Let the blows descend upon my head; but may they leave my faith and hope in God untouched."

Hemangini bowed to me, and touched my feet. "May you be happy," said I, blessing her, "and enjoy unbroken prosperity."

Hemangini was still unsatisfied.

"Dearest sister," she said, "a blessing for me is not enough. You must make our happiness complete. You must, with those saintly hands of yours, accept into your home my husband also. Let me bring him to you."

I said: "Yes, bring him to me."

A few moments later I heard a familiar footstep, and the question, "Kumo, how are you ? "

I started up, and bowed to the ground, and cried: "Dada! "

Hemangini burst out laughing.

"You still call him elder brother?" she asked. "What nonsense! Call him younger brother now, and pull his ears and cease him, for he has married me, your younger sister."

Then I understood. My husband had been saved from that great sin. He had not fallen.

I knew my Dada had determined never to marry. And, since my mother had died, there was no sacred wish of hers to implore him to wedlock. But I, his sister, by my sore need bad brought it to pass. He had married for my sake.

Tears of joy gushed from my eyes, and poured down my cheeks. I tried, but I could not stop them. Dada slowly passed his fingers through my hair. Hemangini clung to me, and went on laughing.

I was lying awake in my bed for the best part of the night, waiting with straining anxiety for my husband's return. I could not imagine how he would bear the shock of shame and disappointment.

When it was long past the hour of midnight, slowly my door opened. I sat up on my bed, and listened. They were the footsteps of my husband. My heart began to beat wildly. He came up to my bed, held my band in his.

"Your Dada," said he, "has saved me from destruction. I was being dragged down and down by a moments madness. An infatuation had seized me, from which I seemed unable to escape. God alone knows what a load I was carrying on that day when I entered the boat. The storm came down on river, and covered the sky. In the midst of all fears I had a secret wish in my heart to be drowned, and so disentangle my life from the knot which I had tied it. I reached

Mathurganj. There I heard the news which set me free. Your brother had married Hemangini. I cannot tell you with what joy and shame I heard it. I hastened on board the boat again. In that moment of self-revelation I knew that I could have no happiness except with you. You are a Goddess."

I laughed and cried at the same time, and said: "No, no, no! I am not going to be a Goddess any longer I am simply your own little wife. I am an ordinary woman."

"Dearest," he replied, "I have also something I want to say to you. Never again put me to shame by calling me your God."

On the next day the little town became joyous with sound of conch shells. But nobody made any reference to that night of madness, when all was so nearly lost.

Living Or Dead?
I

The widow in the house of Saradasankar, the Ranihat zemindar, had no kinsmen of her father's family. One after another all had died. Nor had she in her husband's family any one she could call her own, neither husband nor son. The child of her brother-in-law Saradasankar was her darling. Far a long time after his birth, his mother had been very ill, and the widow, his aunt Kadambini, had fostered him. If a woman fosters another's child, her love for him is all the stronger because she has no claim upon him-no claim of kinship, that is, but simply the claim of love. Love cannot prove its claim by any document which society accepts, and does not wish to prove it; it merely worships with double passion its life's uncertain treasure. Thus all the widow's thwarted love went out to wards this little child. One night in Sraban Kadambini died suddenly. For some reason her heart stopped beating. Everywhere else the world held on its course; only m this gentle little breast, suffering with love, the watch of time stood still forever.

Lest they should be harassed by the poike, four of the zemindar's Brahmin servants took away the body, without ceremony, to be burned. The burning-ground of Ranihat was very far from the village. There was a hut beside a tank, a huge banian near it, and nothing more. Formerly a river, now completely dried up, ran through the ground, and part of the watercourse had been dug out to make a tank for the performance of funeral rites. The people considered the tank as part of the river and reverenced it as such.

Taking the body into the hut, the four men sat down to wait for the wood. The time seemed so long that two of the four grew restless, and went to see why it did not come. Nitai and Gurucharan being gone, Bidhu and Banamali remained to watch over the body.

It was a dark night of Sraban. Heavy clouds hung In a starless sky. The two men sat silent in the dark room. Their matches and lamp were useless. The matches were damp, and would not light, for all their efforts, and the lantern went out.

After a long silence, one said: "Brother, it would be good if we had a bowl of tobacco. In our hurry we brought none."

The other answered: "I can run and bring all we want."

Understanding why Banarnali wanted to go (From fear of ghosts, the burning-ground being considered haunted.), Bidhu said: "I daresay! Meanwhile, I suppose I am to sit here alone!"

Conversation ceased again. Five minutes seemed like an hour. In their minds they cursed the two, who had gone to fetch the wood, and they began to suspect that they sat gossiping in some pleasant nook. There was no sound anywhere, except the incessant noise of frogs and crickets from the tank. Then suddenly they fancied that the bed shook slightly, as if the dead body had turned on its side. Bidhu and Banamali trembled, and began muttering: "Ram, Ram." A deep sigh was heard in the room. In a moment the watchers leapt out of the hut, and raced for the village.

After running aboat three miles, they met their colleagues coming back with a lantern. As a matter of fact, they had gone to smoke, and knew nothing about the wood. But they declared that a tree had been cut down, and that, when it was split up, it would be brought along at once. Then Bidhu and Banamali told them what had happened in the hut. Nitai and Gurucharan scoffed at the story, and abused Bidhu and Banamali angrily for leaving their duty.

Without delay all four returned to the hut. As they entered, they saw at once that the body was gone; nothing but an empty bed remained. They stared at one another. Could a jackal have taken it? But there was no scrap of clothing anywhere. Going outside, they saw that on the mud that had collected at the door of the but there were a woman's tiny footprints, newly made. Saradasankar was no fool, and they could hardly persuade him to believe in this ghost story. So after much discussion the four decided that it would be best to say that the body had been burnt.

Towards dawn, when the men with the wood arrived they were told that, owing to their delay, the work had been done without them; there had been some wood in the but after all. No one was likely to question this, since a dead body is not such a valuable property that any one would steal it.

II

Everyone knows that, even when there is no sign, life is often secretly present, and may begin again in an apparently dead body. Kadambini was not dead; only the machine of her life had for some reason suddenly stopped.

When consciousness returned, she saw dense darkness on all sides. It occurred to her that she was not lying in her usual place. She called out "Sister," but no answer came from the darkness. As she sat up, terror-stricken, she remembered her death-bed, the sudden pain at her breast, the beginning of a choking sensation. Her elder sister-in-law was warming some milk for the child, when Kadambini became faint, and fell on the bed, saying with a choking voice: "Sister, bring the child here. I am worried." After that everything was black, as when an inkpot is upset over an exercise-book. Kadambini's memory and consciousness, all the letters of the world's book, in a moment became formless. The widow could not remember whether the child, in the sweet voice of love, called her " Auntie," as if for the last time, or not; she could not remember whether, as she left the world she knew for death's endless unknown journey, she had received a parting gift of affection, love's passage-money for the silent land. At first, I fancy, she thought the lonely dark place was the House of Yama, where there is nothing to see, nothing to hear, nothing to do, only an eternal watch. But when a cold damp wind drove through the open door, and she heard the croaking of frogs, she remembered vividly and in a moment all the rains of her short life, and could feel her kinship with the earth. Then came a flash of lightning, and she saw the tank, the banian, the great plain, the far-off trees. She remembered how at full moon she had sometimes come to bathe in this tank, and how dreadful death had seemed when she saw a corpse on the burning-ground.

Her first thought was to return home. But then she reflected: "I am dead. How can I return home? That would bring disaster on them. I have left the kingdom of the living; I am my own ghost!" If this were not so, she reasoned, how could she have got out of Saradasankar's well-guarded zenana, and come to this distant burningground at midnight? Also, if her funeral rites had not been finished, where had the men gone who should burn her? Recalling her death-moment in Saradasankar's brightly-lit house, she now found herself alone in a distant, deserted, dark burning. ground. Surely she was no member of earthly society! Surely she was a creature of horror, of ill-omen, her own ghost!

At this thought, all the bonds were snapped which bound her to the world. She felt that she had marvellous strength, endless freedom. She could do what she liked, go where she pleased. Mad with the inspiration of this new idea, she rushed from the but like a gust of wind, and stood upon the burning. ground. All trace of shame or fear had left her.

But as she walked on and on, her feet grew tired, her body weak. The plain stretched on endlessly; here and there were paddy-fields; sometimes she found herself standing knee-deep in water.

At the first glimmer of dawn she heard one or two birds cry from the bamboo-clumps 6y the distant houses. Then terror seized her. She could not tell in what new relation she stood to the earth and to living folk. So long as she had been on the plain, on the burning-ground, covered by the dark night of Sraban, so long she had been fearless, a denizen of her own kingdom. By daylight the homes of men filled her with fear. Men and ghosts dread each other, for their tribes inhabit different banks of the river of death.

III

Her clothes were clotted in the mud; strange thoughts and walking by night had given her the aspect of a madwoman; truly, her apparition was such that folk might have been afraid of her, and children might have stoned her or run away. Luckily, the first to catch sight of her was a traveller. He came up, and said:

"Mother, you look a respectable woman. Wherever are you going, alone and in this guise?"

Kadambini, unable to collect her thoughts, stared at him in silence. She could not think that she was still in touch with the world, that she looked like a respectable woman, that a traveller was asking her questions.

Again the min said: "Come, mother, I will see you home. Tell me where you live."

Kadambini thought. To return to her father-in-law's house would be absurd, and she had no father's house. Then she remembered the friend of her childhood. She had not seen Jogmaya since the days of her youth, but from time to time they had exchanged letters. Occasionally there had been quarrels between them, as was only right, since Kadambini wished to make it dear that her love for Jogmaya was unbounded, while her friend complained that Kadambini did not return a love equal to her own. They were both sure that, if they once met, they would be inseparable.

Kadambini said to the traveller: "I will go to Sripati's house at Nisindapur."

As he was going to Calcutta, Nisindapur, though not near, was on his way. So he took Kadambini to Sripati s house, and the friends met again. At first they did not recognise one another, but gradually each recognised the features of the other's childhood.

"What luck!" said Jogmaya. "I never dreamt that I should see you again. But how hate you come here, sister? Your father-in-law's folk surely didn't let you go!"

Kadambini remained silent, and at last said: "Sister, do not ask about my father-in-law. Give me a corner, and treat me as a servant: I will do your work."

"What?" cried Jogmaya. "Keep you like a servant! Why, you are my closest friend, you are my –" and so on and so on.

Just then Sripati came in. Kadambini stared at him for some time, and then went out very slowly. She kept her head uncovered, and showed not the slightest modesty or respect. Jogmaya, fearing that Sripati would be prejudiced against her friend, began an elaborate explanation. But Sripati, who readily agreed to anything Jogmaya said, cut short her story, and left his wife uneasy in her mind.

Kadambini had come, but she was not at one with her friend: death was between them. She could feel no intimacy for others so long as her existence perplexed her and consciousness remained. Kadambini would look at Jogmaya, and brood. She would think: "She has her husband and her work, she lives in a world far away from mine. She shares affection and duty with the people of the world; I am an empty shadow. She is among the living; I am in eternity."

Jogmaya also was uneasy, but could not explain why. Women do not love mystery, because, though uncertainty may be transmuted into poetry, into heroism, into scholarship, it cannot be turned to account in household work. So, when a woman cannot understand a thing, she either destroys and forgets it, or she shapes it anew for her own use; if she fails to deal with it in one of these ways, she loses her temper with it. The greater Kadambini's abstraction became, the more impatient was Jogmaya with her, wondering what trouble weighed upon her mind.

Then a new danger arose. Kadambini was afraid of herself; yet she could not flee from herself. Those who fear ghosts fear those who are behind them; wherever they cannot see there is fear. But Kadambini's chief terror lay in herself, for she dreaded nothing external. At the dead of night, when alone in her room, she screamed; in the evening, when she saw her shadow in the lamp-light, her whole body shook. Watching her fearfulness, the rest of the house fell into a sort of terror. The servants and Jogmaya herself began to see ghosts.

One midnight, Kadambini came out from her bedroom weeping, and wailed at Jogmaya's door: "Sister, sister, let me lie at your feet! Do not put me by myself!"

Jogmaya's anger was no less than her fear. She would have liked to drive Kadambini from the house that very second. The good-natured Sripati, after much effort, succeeded in quieting their guest, and put her in the next room.

Next day Sripati was unexpectedly summoned to his wife's apartments. She began to upbraid him: "You, do you call yourself a man? A woman runs away from her father-in-law, and enters your house; a month passes, and you haven't hinted that she should go away, nor have I heard the slightest protest from you. I should cake it as a favour if you would explain yourself. You men are all alike."

Men, as a race, have a natural partiality for womankind in general, foe which women themselves hold them accountable.   Although Sripati was prepared to touch Jogmaya's body, and swear that his kind feeling towards the helpless but beautiful Kadambini was no whit greater than it should be, he could not prove it by his behaviour. He thought that her father-in-law's people must have treated this forlorn widow abominably, if she could bear it no longer, and was driven to take refuge with him. As she had neither father nor mother, how could he desert her? So saying, he let the matter drop, far he had no mind to distress Kadambini by asking her unpleasant questions.

His wife, then, tried other means of her sluggish lord, until at last he saw that for the sake of peace he must send word to Kadambini's father-in-law. The result of a letter, he thought, might not be satisfactory; so he resolved to go to Ranihat, and act on what he learnt.

So Sripati went, and Jogmaya on her part said to Kadambini "Friend, it hardly seems proper for you to stop here any longer. What will people say? "

Kadambini stared solemnly at Jogmaya, and said: "What have I to do with people?"

Jogmaya was astounded. Then she said sharply: "If you have nothing to do with people, we have. How can we explain the detention of a woman belonging to another house?"

Kadambini said: "Where is my father-in-law's house?"

"Confound it!" thought Jogmaya. "What will the wretched woman say next?"

Very slowly Kadambini said: "What have I to do with you? Am I of the earth? You laugh, weep, love; each grips and holds his own; I merely look. You are human, I a shadow. I cannot understand why God has kept me in this world of yours."

So strange were her look and speech that Jogmaya understood something of her drift, though not all. Unable either to dismiss her, or to ask her any more questions, she went away, oppressed with thought.

IV

It was nearly ten o'clock at night when Sripati returned from Ranihat. The earth was drowned in torrents of rain. It seemed that the downpour would never stop, that the night would never end.

Jogmaya asked: "Well?"

"I've lots to say, presently."

So saying, Sripati changed his clothes, and sat down to supper; then he lay dawn for a smoke. His mind was perplexed.

His wife stilled her curiosity for a long time; then she came to his couch and demanded: "What did you hear?"

"That you have certainly made a mistake."

Jogmaya was nettled. Women never make mistakes, or, if they do, a sensible man never mentions them; it is better to take them on his own shoulders. Jogmaya snapped: "May I be permitted to hear how?"

Sripati replied: "The woman you have taken into your house is not your Kadambini."

Hearing this, she was greatly annoyed, especially since it was her husband who said it. "What! I don't know my own friend? I must come to you to recognise her! You are clever, indeed!"

Sripati explained that there was no need to quarrel about his cleverness. He could prove what he said. There was no doubt that Jogmaya's Kadambini was dead.

Jogmaya replied: "Listen! You've certainly made some huge mistake. You've been to the wrong house, or are confused as to what you have heard. Who told you to go yourself? Write a letter, and everything will be cleared up."

Sripati was hurt by his wife's lack of faith in his executive ability; he produced all sorts of proof, without result. Midnight found them still asserting and contradicting. Although they were both agreed now that Kadambini should be got out of the house, although Sripati believed that their guest had deceived his wife all the time by a pretended acquaintance, and Jogmaya that she was a prostitute, yet in the present discussion neither would acknowledge defeat. By degrees their voices became so loud that they forgot that Kadambini was sleeping in the next room.

The one said: "We're in a nice fix! I tell you, I heard it with my own ears!" And the other answered angrily: "What do I care about that? I can see with my own eyes, surely."

At length Jogmaya said: "Very well. Tell me when Kadambini died." She thought that if she could find a discrepancy between the day of death and the date of some letter from Kadambini, she could prove that Sripati erred.

He told her the date of Kadambini's death, and they both saw that it fell on the very day before she came to their house. Jogmaya's heart trembled, even Sripati was not unmoved.

Just then the door flew open; a damp wind swept in and blew the lamp out. The darkness rushed after it, and filled the whole house. Kadambini stood in the room. It was nearly one o'clock, the rain was pelting outside.

Kadambini spoke: "Friend, I am your Kadambini, but I am no longer living. I am dead."

Jogmaya screamed with terror; Sripati could speak.

"But, save in being dead, I have done you no wrong. If I have no place among the living, I have none among the dead. Oh! whither shall I go?"

Crying as if to wake the sleeping Creator in the dense night of rain, she asked again: " Oh! whither shall I go? "

So saying Kadambini left her friend fainting in the dark house, and went out into the world, seeking her own place.

V

It is hard to say how Kadambini reached Ranihat. At first she showed herself to no one, but spent the whole day in a ruined temple, starving. When the untimely afternoon of the rains was pitch-black, and people huddled into their houses for fear of the impending storm, then Kadambini came forth. Her heart trembled as she reached her father-in- law's house; and when, drawing a thick veil over her face, she entered, none of the doorkeepers objected, since they took her for a servant. And the rain was pouring down, and the wind howled.

The mistress, Saradasankar's wife, was playing cards with her widowed sister. A servant was in the kitchen, the sick child was sleeping in the bedroom. Kadambini, escaping every one's notice, entered this room. I do not know why she had come to her father-in-law's house; she herself did not know; she felt only that she wanted to see her child again. She had no thought where to go next, or what to do.

In the lighted room she saw the child sleeping, his fists clenched, his body wasted with fever. At sight of him, her heart became parched and thirsty. If only she could press that tortured body to her breast! Immediately the thought followed: "I do not exist. Who would see it? His mother loves company, loves gossip and cards. All the time that she left me in charge, she was herself free from anxiety, nor was she troubled about him in the least. Who will look after him now as I did?"

The child turned on his side, and cried, half-asleep: "Auntie, give me water." Her darling had not yet forgotten his auntie! In a fever of excitement, she poured out some water, and, taking him to her breast, she gave it him.

As long as he was asleep, the child felt no strangeness in taking water from the accustomed hand. But when Kadambini satisfied her long-starved longing, and kissed him and began rocking him asleep again, he awoke and embraced her. "Did you die, Auntie?" he asked.

"Yes, darling."

"And you have come back? Do not die again."

Before she could answer disaster overtook her. One of the maidservants coming in with a cup of sago dropped it, and fell down. At the crash the mistress left her cards, and entered the room. She stood like a pillar of wood, unable to flee or speak. Seeing all this, the child, too, became terrified, and burst out weeping: " Go away, Auntie," he said, "go away!"

Now at last Kadambini understood that she had not died. The old room, the old things, the same child, the same love, all returned to their living state, without change or difference between her and them. In her friend's house she had felt that her childhood's companion was dead. In her child's room she knew that the boy's "Auntie" was not dead at all. In anguished tones she said: "Sister, why do you dread me? See, I am as you knew me."

Her sister-in-law could endure no longer, and fell into a faint. Saradasankar himself entered the zenana. With folded hands, he said piteously: "Is this right? Satis is my only son. Why do you show yourself to him? Are we not your own kin? Since you went, he has wasted away daily; his fever has been incessant; day and night he cries: `Auntie, Auntie.' You have left the world; break these bonds of maya (Illusory affection binding a soul to the world). We will perform all funeral honours."

Kadambini could bear no more. She said: "Oh, I am not dead, I am not dead. Oh, how can I persuade you that I am not dead? I am living, living!" She lifted a brass pot from the ground and dashed it against her forehead. The blood ran from her brow. "Look!" she cried, "I am living!" Saradasankar stood like an image; the child screamed with fear, the two fainting women lay still.

Then Kadambini, shouting "I am not dead, I am not dead," went down the steps to the zenana well, and plunged in. From the upper storey Saradasankar heard the splash.

All night the rain poured; it poured next day at dawn, was pouring still at noon. By dying, Kadambini had given proof that she was not dead.

The Hungry Stones

My kinsman and myself were returning to Calcutta from our Puja trip when we met the man in a train. From his dress and bearing we took him at first for an up-country Mahomedan, but we were puzzled as we heard him talk. He discoursed upon all subjects so confidently that you might think the Disposer of All Things consulted him at all times in all that He did. Hitherto we had been perfectly happy, as we did not know that secret and unheard-of forces were at work, that the Russians had advanced close to us, that the English had deep and secret policies, that confusion among the native chiefs had come to a head. But our newly-acquired friend said with a sly smile: "There happen more things in heaven and earth, Horatio, than are reported in your newspapers." As we had never stirred out of our homes before, the demeanour of the man struck us dumb with wonder. Be the topic ever so trivial, he would quote science, or comment on the Vedas, or repeat quatrains from some Persian poet; and as we had no pretence to a knowledge of science or the Vedas or Persian, our admiration for him went on increasing, and my kinsman, a theosophist, was firmly convinced that our fellow-passenger must have been supernaturally inspired by some strange magnetism" or "occult power," by an "astral body" or something of that kind. He listened to the tritest saying that fell from the lips of our extraordinary companion with devotional rapture, and secretly took down notes of his conversation. I fancy that the extraordinary man saw this, and was a little pleased with it.

When the train reached the junction, we assembled in the waiting room for the connection. It was then 10 P.M., and as the train, we heard, was likely to be very late, owing to something wrong in the lines, I spread my bed on the table and was about to lie down for a comfortable doze, when the extraordinary person deliberately set about spinning the following yarn. Of course, I could get no sleep that night.

When, owing to a disagreement about some questions of administrative policy, I threw up my post at Junagarh, and entered the service of the Nizam of Hydria, they appointed me at once, as a strong young man, collector of cotton duties at Barich.

Barich is a lovely place. The Susta "chatters over stony ways and babbles on the pebbles," tripping, like a skilful dancing girl, in through the woods below the lonely hills. A flight of 150 steps rises from the river, and above that flight, on the river's brim and at the foot of the hills, there stands a solitary marble palace. Around it there is no habitation of man, the village and the cotton mart of Barich being far off.

About 250 years ago the Emperor Mahmud Shah II. had built this lonely palace for his pleasure and luxury. In his days jets of rose-water spurted from its fountains, and on the cold marble floors of its spray- cooled rooms young Persian damsels would sit, their hair dishevelled before bathing, and, splashing their soft naked feet in the clear water of the reservoirs, would sing, to the tune of the guitar, the ghazals of their vineyards.

The fountains play no longer; the songs have ceased; no longer do snow-white feet step gracefully on the snowy marble. It is but the vast and solitary quarters of cess-collectors like us, men oppressed with solitude and deprived of the society of women. Now, Karim Khan, the old clerk of my office, warned me repeatedly not to take up my abode there. "Pass the day there, if you like," said he, "but never stay the night." I passed it off with a light laugh. The servants said that they would work till dark and go away at night. I gave my ready assent. The house had such a bad name that even thieves would not venture near it after dark.

At first the solitude of the deserted palace weighed upon me like a nightmare. I would stay out, and work hard as long as possible, then return home at night jaded and tired, go to bed and fall asleep.

Before a week had passed, the place began to exert a weird fascination upon me. It is difficult to describe or to induce people to believe; but I felt as if the whole house was like a living organism slowly and imperceptibly digesting me by the action of some stupefying gastric juice.

Perhaps the process had begun as soon as I set my foot in the house, but I distinctly remember the day on which I first was conscious of it.

It was the beginning of summer, and the market being dull I had no work to do. A little before sunset I was sitting in an arm-chair near the water's edge below the steps. The Susta had shrunk and sunk low; a broad patch of sand on the other side glowed with the hues of evening; on this side the pebbles at the bottom of the clear shallow waters were glistening. There was not a breath of wind anywhere, and the still air was laden with an oppressive scent from the spicy shrubs growing on the hills close by.

As the sun sank behind the hill-tops a long dark curtain fell upon the stage of day, and the intervening hills cut short the time in which light and shade mingle at sunset. I thought of going out for a ride, and was about to get up when I heard a footfall on the steps behind. I looked back, but there was no one.

As I sat down again, thinking it to be an illusion, I heard many footfalls, as if a large number of persons were rushing down the steps. A strange thrill of delight, slightly tinged with fear, passed through my frame, and though there was not a figure before my eyes, methought I saw a bevy of joyous maidens coming down the steps to bathe in the Susta in that summer evening. Not a sound was in the valley, in the river, or in the palace, to break the silence, but I distinctly heard the maidens' gay and mirthful laugh, like the gurgle of a spring gushing forth in a hundred cascades, as they ran past me, in quick playful pursuit of each other, towards the river, without noticing me at all. As they were invisible to me, so I was, as it were, invisible to them. The river was perfectly calm, but I felt that its still, shallow, and clear waters were stirred suddenly by the splash of many an arm jingling with bracelets, that the girls laughed and dashed and spattered water at one another, that the feet of the fair swimmers tossed the tiny waves up in showers of pearl.

I felt a thrill at my heart, I cannot say whether the excitement was due to fear or delight or curiosity. I had a strong desire to see them more clearly, but naught was visible before me; I thought I could catch all that they said if I only strained my ears; but however hard I strained them, I heard nothing but the chirping of the cicadas in the woods. It seemed as if a dark curtain of 250 years was hanging before me, and I would fain lift a corner of it tremblingly and peer through, though the assembly on the other side was completely enveloped in darkness.

The oppressive closeness of the evening was broken by a sudden gust of wind, and the still surface of the Suista rippled and curled like the hair of a nymph, and from the woods wrapt in the evening gloom there came forth a simultaneous murmur, as though they were awakening from a black dream. Call it reality or dream, the momentary glimpse of that invisible mirage reflected from a far-off world, 250 years old, vanished in a flash. The mystic forms that brushed past me with their quick unbodied steps, and loud, voiceless laughter, and threw themselves into the river, did not go back wringing their dripping robes as they went. Like fragrance wafted away by the wind they were dispersed by a single breath of the spring.

Then I was filled with a lively fear that it was the Muse that had taken advantage of my solitude and possessed me - the witch had evidently come to ruin a poor devil like myself making a living by collecting cotton duties. I decided to have a good dinner, it is the empty stomach that all sorts of incurable diseases find an easy prey. I sent for my cook and gave orders for a rich, sumptuous moghlai dinner, redolent of spices and ghi.

Next morning the whole affair appeared a queer fantasy. With a light heart I put on a sola hat like the sahebs, and drove out to my work. I was to have written my quarterly report that day, and expected to return late; but before it was dark I was strangely drawn to my house, by what I could not say, I felt they were all waiting, and that I should delay no longer. Leaving my report unfinished I rose, put on my sola hat, and startling the dark, shady, desolate path with the rattle of my carriage, I reached the vast silent palace standing on the gloomy skirts of the hills.

On the first floor the stairs led to a very spacious hall, its roof stretching wide over ornamental arches resting on three rows of massive pillars, and groaning day and night under the weight of its own intense solitude. The day had just closed, and the lamps had not yet been lighted. As I pushed the door open a great bustle seemed to follow within, as if a throng of people had broken up in confusion, and rushed out through the doors and windows and corridors and verandas and rooms, to make its hurried escape.

As I saw no one I stood bewildered, my hair on end in a kind of ecstatic delight, and a faint scent of attar and unguents almost effected by age lingered in my nostrils. Standing in the darkness of that vast desolate hall between the rows of those ancient pillars, I could hear the gurgle of fountains plashing on the marble floor, a strange tune on the guitar, the jingle of ornaments and the tinkle of anklets, the clang of bells tolling the hours, the distant note of nahabat, the din of the crystal pendants of chandeliers shaken by the breeze, the song of bulbuls from the cages in the corridors, the cackle of storks in the gardens, all creating round me a strange unearthly music.

Then I came under such a spell that this intangible, inaccessible, unearthly vision appeared to be the only reality in the world and all else a mere dream. That I, that is to say, Srijut So-and-so, the eldest son of So-and-so of blessed memory, should be drawing a monthly salary of Rs. 450 by the discharge of my duties as collector of cotton duties, and driving in my dog-cart to my office every day in a short coat and soia hat, appeared to me to be such an astonishingly ludicrous illusion that I burst into a horse-laugh, as I stood in the gloom of that vast silent hall.

At that moment my servant entered with a lighted kerosene lamp in his hand. I do not know whether he thought me mad, but it came back to me at once that I was in very deed Srijut So-and-so, son of So-and-so of blessed memory, and that, while our poets, great and small, alone could say whether inside of or outside the earth there was a region where unseen fountains perpetually played and fairy guitars, struck by invisible fingers, sent forth an eternal harmony, this at any rate was certain, that I collected duties at the cotton market at Banch, and earned thereby Rs. 450 per mensem as my salary. I laughed in great glee at my curious illusion, as I sat over the newspaper at my camp-table, lighted by the kerosene lamp.

After I had finished my paper and eaten my moghlai dinner, I put out the lamp, and lay down on my bed in a small side-room. Through the open window a radiant star, high above the Avalli hills skirted by the darkness of their woods, was gazing intently from millions and millions of miles away in the sky at Mr. Collector lying on a humble camp- bedstead. I wondered and felt amused at the idea, and do not knew when I fell asleep or how long I slept; but I suddenly awoke with a start, though I heard no sound and saw no intruder, only the steady bright star on the hilltop had set, and the dim light of the new moon was stealthily entering the room through the open window, as if ashamed of its intrusion.

I saw nobody, but felt as if someone was gently pushing me. As I awoke she said not a word, but beckoned me with her five fingers bedecked with rings to follow her cautiously. I got up noiselessly, and, though not a soul save myself was there in the countless apartments of that deserted palace with its slumbering sounds and waiting echoes, I feared at every step lest anyone should wake up. Most of the rooms of the palace were always kept closed, and I had never entered them.

I followed breathless and with silent steps my invisible guide, I cannot now say where. What endless dark and narrow passages, what long corridors, what silent and solemn audience-chambers and close secret cells I crossed!

Though I could not see my fair guide, her form was not invisible to my mind's eye, an Arab girl, her arms, hard and smooth as marble, visible through her loose sleeves, a thin veil falling on her face from the fringe of her cap, and a curved dagger at her waist! Methought that one of the thousand and one Arabian Nights had been wafted to me from the world of romance, and that at the dead of night I was wending my way through the dark narrow alleys of slumbering Bagdad to a trysting-place fraught with peril.

At last my fair guide stopped abruptly before a deep blue screen, and seemed to point to something below. There was nothing there, but a sudden dread froze the blood in my heart-methought I saw there on the floor at the foot of the screen a terrible negro eunuch dressed in rich brocade, sitting and dozing with outstretched legs, with a naked sword on his lap. My fair guide lightly tripped over his legs and held up a fringe of the screen. I could catch a glimpse of a part of the room spread with a Persian carpet, some onewas sitting inside on a bed, I could not see her, but only caught a glimpse of two exquisite feet in gold-embroidered slippers, hanging out from loose saffron-coloured paijamas and placed idly on the orange-coloured velvet carpet. On one side there was a bluish crystal tray on which a few apples, pears, oranges, and bunches of grapes in plenty, two small cups and a gold- tinted decanter were evidently waiting the guest. A fragrant intoxicating vapour, issuing from a strange sort of incense that burned within, almost overpowered my senses.

As with trembling heart I made an attempt to step across the outstretched legs of the eunuch, he woke up suddenly with a start, and the sword fell from his lap with a sharp clang on the marble floor. A terrific scream made me jump, and I saw I was sitting on that camp- bedstead of mine sweating heavily; and the crescent moon looked pale in the morning light like a weary sleepless patient at dawn; and our crazy Meher Ali was crying out, as is his daily custom, "Stand back! Stand back!!" while he went along the lonely road.

Such was the abrupt close of one of my Arabian Nights; but there were yet a thousand nights left.

Then followed a great discord between my days and nights. During the day I would go to my work worn and tired, cursing the bewitching night and her empty dreams, but as night came my daily life with its bonds and shackles of work would appear a petty, false, ludicrous vanity.

After nightfall I was caught and overwhelmed in the snare of a strange intoxication, I would then be transformed into some unknown personage of a bygone age, playing my part in unwritten history; and my short English coat and tight breeches did not suit me in the least. With a red velvet cap on my head, loose paijamas, an embroidered vest, a long flowing silk gown, and coloured handkerchiefs scented with attar, I would complete my elaborate toilet, sit on a high-cushioned chair, and replace my cigarette with a many-coiled narghileh filled with rose-water, as if in eager expectation of a strange meeting with the beloved one.

I have no power to describe the marvellous incidents that unfolded themselves, as the gloom of the night deepened. I felt as if in the curious apartments of that vast edifice the fragments of a beautiful story, which I could follow for some distance, but of which I could never see the end, flew about in a sudden gust of the vernal breeze. And all the same I would wander from room to room in pursuit of them the whole night long.

Amid the eddy of these dream-fragments, amid the smell of henna and the twanging of the guitar, amid the waves of air charged with fragrant spray, I would catch like a flash of lightning the momentary glimpse of a fair damsel. She it was who had saffron-coloured paijamas, white ruddy soft feet in gold-embroidered slippers with curved toes, a close- fitting bodice wrought with gold, a red cap, from which a golden frill fell on her snowy brow and cheeks.

She had maddened me. In pursuit of her I wandered from room to room, from path to path among the bewildering maze of alleys in the enchanted dreamland of the nether world of sleep.

Sometimes in the evening, while arraying myself carefully as a prince of the blood-royal before a large mirror, with a candle burning on either side, I would see a sudden reflection of the Persian beauty by the side of my own. A swift turn of her neck, a quick eager glance of intense passion and pain glowing in her large dark eyes, just a suspicion of speech on her dainty red lips, her figure, fair and slim crowned with youth like a blossoming creeper, quickly uplifted in her graceful tilting gait, a dazzling flash of pain and craving and ecstasy, a smile and a glance and a blaze of jewels and silk, and she melted away. A wild glist of wind, laden with all the fragrance of hills and woods, would put out my light, and I would fling aside my dress and lie down on my bed, my eyes closed and my body thrilling with delight, and there around me in the breeze, amid all the perfume of the woods and hills, floated through the silent gloom many a caress and many a kiss and many a tender touch of hands, and gentle murmurs in my ears, and fragrant breaths on my brow; or a sweetly-perfumed kerchief was wafted again and again on my cheeks. Then slowly a mysterious serpent would twist her stupefying coils about me; and heaving a heavy sigh, I would lapse into insensibility, and then into a profound slumber.

One evening I decided to go out on my horse, I do not know who implored me to stay-but I would listen to no entreaties that day. My English hat and coat were resting on a rack, and I was about to take them down when a sudden whirlwind, crested with the sands of the Susta and the dead leaves of the Avalli hills, caught them up, and whirled them round and round, while a loud peal of merry laughter rose higher and higher, striking all the chords of mirth till it died away in the land of sunset.

I could not go out for my ride, and the next day I gave up my queer English coat and hat for good.

That day again at dead of night I heard the stifled heart-breaking sobs of someone, as if below the bed, below the floor, below the stony foundation of that gigantic palace, from the depths of a dark damp grave, a voice piteously cried and implored me: "Oh, rescue me! Break through these doors of hard illusion, deathlike slumber and fruitless dreams, place by your side on the saddle, press me to your heart, and, riding through hills and woods and across the river, take me to the warm radiance of your sunny rooms above!"

Who am I? Oh, how can I rescue thee? What drowning beauty, what incarnate passion shall I drag to the shore from this wild eddy of dreams? O lovely ethereal apparition! Where didst thou flourish and when?" By what cool spring, under the shade of what date-groves, wast thou born, in the lap of what homeless wanderer in the desert? What Bedouin snatched thee from thy mother's arms, an opening bud plucked from a wild creeper, placed thee on a horse swift as lightning, crossed the burning sands, and took thee to the slave-market of what royal city? And there, what officer of the Badshah, seeing the glory of thy bashful blossoming youth, paid for thee in gold, placed thee in a golden palanquin, and offered thee as a present for the seraglio of his master? And O, the history of that place! The music of the sareng, the jingle of anklets, the occasional flash of daggers and the glowing wine of Shiraz poison, and the piercing flashing glance! What infinite grandeur, what endless servitude!

The slave-girls to thy right and left waved the chamar as diamonds flashed from their bracelets; the Badshah, the king of kings, fell on his knees at thy snowy feet in bejewelled shoes, and outside the terrible Abyssinian eunuch, looking like a messenger of death, but clothed like an angel, stood with a naked sword in his hand! Then, O, thou flower of the desert, swept away by the blood-stained dazzling ocean of grandeur, with its foam of jealousy, its rocks and shoals of intrigue, on what shore of cruel death wast thou cast, or in what other land more splendid and more cruel?

Suddenly at this moment that crazy Meher Ali screamed out: "Stand back! Stand back!! All is false! All is false!!" I opened my eyes and saw that it was already light. My chaprasi came and handed me my letters, and the cook waited with a salam for my orders.

I said; "No, I can stay here no longer." That very day I packed up, and moved to my office. Old Karim Khan smiled a little as he saw me. I felt nettled, but said nothing, and fell to my work.

As evening approached I grew absent-minded; I felt as if I had an appointment to keep; and the work of examining the cotton accounts seemed wholly useless; even the Nizamat of the Nizam did not appear to be of much worth. Whatever belonged to the present, whatever was moving and acting and working for bread seemed trivial, meaningless, and contemptible.

I threw my pen down, closed my ledgers, got into my dog-cart, and drove away. I noticed that it stopped of itself at the gate of the marble palace just at the hour of twilight. With quick steps I climbed the stairs, and entered the room.

A heavy silence was reigning within. The dark rooms were looking sullen as if they had taken offence. My heart was full of contrition, but there was no one to whom I could lay it bare, or of whom I could ask forgiveness. I wandered about the dark rooms with a vacant mind. I wished I had a guitar to which I could sing to the unknown: "O fire, the poor moth that made a vain effort to fly away has come back to thee! Forgive it but this once, burn its wings and consume it in thy flame!"

Suddenly two tear-drops fell from overhead on my brow. Dark masses of clouds overcast the top of the Avalli hills that day. The gloomy woods and the sooty waters of the Susta were waiting in terrible suspense and in an ominous calm. Suddenly land, water, and sky shivered, and a wild tempest-blast rushed howling through the distant pathless woods, showing its lightning-teeth like a raving maniac who had broken his chains. The desolate halls of the palace banged their doors, and moaned in the bitterness of anguish.

The servants were all in the office, and there was no one to light the lamps. The night was cloudy and moonless. In the dense gloom within I could distinctly feel that a woman was lying on her face on the carpet below the bed, clasping and tearing her long dishevelled hair with desperate fingers. Blood was tricking down her fair brow, and she was now laughing a hard, harsh, mirthless laugh, now bursting into violent wringing sobs, now rending her bodice and striking at her bare bosom, as the wind roared in through the open window, and the rain poured in torrents and soaked her through and through.

All night there was no cessation of the storm or of the passionate cry. I wandered from room to room in the dark, with unavailing sorrow. Whom could I console when no one was by? Whose was this intense agony of sorrow? Whence arose this inconsolable grief?

And the mad man cried out: "Stand back! Stand back!! All is false! All is false!!"

I saw that the day had dawned, and Meher Ali was going round and round the palace with his usual cry in that dreadful weather. Suddenly it came to me that perhaps he also had once lived in that house, and that, though he had gone mad, he came there every day, and went round and round, fascinated by the weird spell cast by the marble demon.

Despite the storm and rain I ran to him and asked: "Ho, Meher Ali, what is false?"

The man answered nothing, but pushing me aside went round and round with his frantic cry, like a bird flying fascinated about the jaws of a snake, and made a desperate effort to warn himself by repeating: "Stand back! Stand back!! All is false! All is false!!"

I ran like a mad man through the pelting rain to my office, and asked Karim Khan: "Tell me the meaning of all this!"

What I gathered from that old man was this: That at one time countless unrequited passions and unsatisfied longings and lurid flames of wild blazing pleasure raged within that palace, and that the curse of all the heart-aches and blasted hopes had made its every stone thirsty and hungry, eager to swallow up like a famished ogress any living man who might chance to approach. Not one of those who lived there for three consecutive nights could escape these cruel jaws, save Meher Ali, who had escaped at the cost of his reason.

I asked: "Is there no means whatever of my release?" The old man said: "There is only one means, and that is very difficult. I will tell you what it is, but first you must hear the history of a young Persian girl who once lived in that pleasure-dome. A stranger or a more bitterly heart-rending tragedy was never enacted on this earth."

Just at this moment the coolies announced that the train was coming. So soon? We hurriedly packed up our luggage, as the tram steamed in. An English gentleman, apparently just aroused from slumber, was looking out of a first-class carriage endeavouring to read the name of the station. As soon as he caught sight of our fellow-passenger, he cried, "Hallo," and took him into his own compartment. As we got into a second-class carriage, we had no chance of finding out who the man was nor what was the end of his story.

I said; "The man evidently took us for fools and imposed upon us out of fun. The story is pure fabrication from start to finish." The discussion that followed ended in a lifelong rupture between my theosophist kinsman and myself.

Rabindranath Tagore: A Biography

Rabindranath Tagore (1861-1941) is an Indian poet, playwright, novelist, composer, painter and a national icon of his country. His profuse literary production ranges from collections of poems such as *Manasi* (1890), *Gitanjali* (1910) and Patraput (1936) to drama such as *Visarjan* (1890), *Raja* (1910), *Muktadhara* (1922) and *Chandalika* (1938) and even numerous musical compositions and songs. In addition, Tagore's publications include a number of novels and several volumes of short stories including his widely appreciated *Gora* (1910) along with *Chaturanga* (1916) and *Ghare-Baire* (1916). The latter is one of his works that were adapted to cinema.

Born in Calcutta, India, to a well-off family, Rabindranath Tagore was raised and educated mainly by servants. His father Devendranath Tagore is a saint and a religious leader of the Adi Dham faith and the Brahmo sect founded by the family's patriarchs. Young Rabindranath Tagore's home was animated by discussions of literary publications, arts, theatrical performances and classical music where most of his 14 siblings were much interested in arts, poetry, music, philosophy and theatre, such as his older sister, Swarnakumari Devi, the renowned Indian novelist, poet and musician.

In addition to such a supportive environment for artistic appreciation and creativity, Tagore's father made him discover language, literature, history and poetry, taking him for long journeys around the country. In 1873, they both left home for the hill station at Dalhousie. Named after the British Governor-General Lord Dalhousie who used to visit it during his summer holidays, the station is surrounded by captivating green hills and heaven-like vistas. During the months spent there, Tagore must have found in the station's assortments of Hindu art and temples, along with the European architecture of its summer residences, a magnificent blending of East and West.

Readers of Tagore's poetry, novels and short stories, such as "The Fruitseller from Kabul," to name but a sample, can surely detect in their imagery and emotional outlets the influence of Dalhousie's breath-taking sceneries and verdure. Tagore's journey with his father was mainly meant to be a necessary stage towards intellectual and moral maturity and individuation. The lessons that the father transmitted to the son in such an inspirational spot were not only meant to be informational lessons but also spiritual ones. Indeed, being a very respected spiritual figure who wished to hand on the torch to younger disciples, Tagore's father inculcated in him mystical yearnings for spiritual knowledge and existential meaning.

It is, however, noteworthy that despite his conspicuous lust for knowledge, Tagore hated the "yoke" of formal education and thought that classroom teaching could only muffle young people's innate and instinctive thirst for discovery and adventure. The two long journeys that he had with his father only reinforced this attitude as they helped nourish his love for nature and the divine. Helped by his father, his brother Hemendranath and the house servants, Tagore studied language, literature, mathematics, geography and history and practiced different sports at home and in the family's manor. When his father sent him to London to study law in 1878, he quickly left University College London and chose to study language, literature and music by himself. Two years later, he travelled back to India without getting the formal degree he was sent for.

Tagore expressed in many an occasion his belief that teaching should arouse curiosity rather than be informative and he strove to put his ideas into practice particularly by founding the Visva-Bharati school, which has now become the Visva-Bharati University, where he established the "brahmacharya" educational system. The main characteristic of Tagore's educational conception was to have teachers incite their students to discover and learn through employing intellectual and spiritual motivational strategies.

As for his writings, Tagore was a genuine prodigy who started weaving his earliest verses by the age of eight in the family's Calcutta residence. A few years later, he pseudonymously published his first collection of poems which was an astounding success to the point that local critics thought the compilation to belong to the 17th-century poet Bhānusimha. He soon shifted to writing short stories and plays to achieve considerable fame in the region. While all his writings were in his native Bengali language, he eventually decided to address Western readers by translating some of his own works into English.

The English versions of his poetic works such as *Manasi* (1890), *Gitimalya* (1914) and mainly what is today considered in the West as his magnum opus, *Gitanjali* (1910), quickly gained ground among Western literary circles. Such works were read, reviewed and prefaced by leading literary figures of the time like William Butler Yeats and Ezra Pound. Tagore soon became an oriental icon who stands for India's literary, spiritual and cultural heritage. In 1913, the relatively small part of his works discovered by the West earned him the Nobel Prize in Literature. In 1915, he was also knighted by the British Crown for his literary achievements.

Once famous in the West, Tagore toured Britain and the United States and lectured in many other European and non-European countries to meet and interact with important celebrities around the world including the celebrated German-born physicist Albert Einstein, Thomas Mann, George Bernard Shaw and H.G. Wells, among many others.

Politically, while Tagore's commitment manifested in his harsh criticism of nationalist extremism and in his avant-garde and reformatory positions at home, he denounced imperialism and advocated universalism and internationalism in the world. In India, he was known for his rejection of the culture of victimhood and for inciting his countrymen to have the courage of assuming the responsibilities of their misfortunes. He saw that salvation could only be realized through education and self-help. In addition to that, Tagore was also socially active in his homeland, supporting students and the poor. As for foreign affairs, Tagore denounced British colonialism and even renounced the honor previously granted by the British Crown in protest against the 1919 Jallianwala Bagh massacre.

Such political views were explicitly expressed in some of Tagore's writings and musical compositions, two of which were chosen by India and Bangladesh as national anthems. His friend Mahatma Gandhi, the celebrated leader of the Indian nationalist movement, expressed his appreciation of these compositions and was said to favor the "Ekla Chalo Re" hymn.

Towards the twilight of his career, Tagore developed new interests, mainly in arts, paintings and sciences. This is mainly expressed in stories like *Se* (1937) and *Tin Sangi* (1940) as well as in his collection of essays entitled *Visva-Parichay* (1937) which represents a literary man's exploration of the fields of astronomy, physics and biology. He even took up drawing and painting at a late age and organized exhibitions of his works in Paris and other cities.
Towards the end of the 1930s, old Rabindranath Tagore's health started to deteriorate until he died on August 7th, 1941, leaving a gigantic oeuvre of numerous volumes of fine poetry, hundreds of texts, short stories, novels, plays, paintings, doodles, more than two thousand songs, two autobiographies and numerous travelogues, essays and lectures.

Tagore's life experience had taught him that divisions between human beings are nothing but an unpleasant mirage. Generally, his oeuvre invites and incites its readers to the exploration of the Other, the exploration of the Self. The following extract from his masterpiece *Gitanjali* may serve as a perfect illustration of Tagore's philosophical vision:

The time that my journey takes is long and the way of it long.

I came out on the chariot of the first gleam of light, and pursued my voyage through the wildernesses of worlds leaving my track on many a star and planet. It is the most distant course that comes nearest to thyself, and that training is the most intricate which leads to the utter simplicity of a tune.

The traveller has to knock at every alien door to come to his own, and one has to wander through all the outer worlds to reach the innermost shrine at the end. My eyes strayed far and wide before I shut them and said 'Here art thou!'

The question and the cry 'Oh, where?' melt into tears of a thousand streams and deluge the world with the flood of the assurance 'I am!' (Song XII)

www.ingramcontent.com/pod-product-compliance
Lightning Source LLC
Chambersburg PA
CBHW061458170626
46811CB00004B/1574